D1087917

IVAN THE FOOL
and other tales of

LEO TOLSTOY

selected and translated by GUY DANIELS

illustrated by DES ASMUSSEN

THE MACMILLAN COMPANY, NEW YORK

To my son,
Matthew Emmet Daniels

The Macmillan Company, New York
Collier-Macmillan Canada, Ltd., Toronto, Ontario
Library of Congress catalog card number: 66-10285
Printed in the United States of America
First Printing

Contents

LEO TOLSTOY

A
Prisoner in the
Caucasus

A Russian gentleman named Zhilin was serving as an army officer in the Caucasus. One day he received a letter from home—from his mother, who was an old woman. In it she said:

I have grown old, and I want to see my beloved son before I die. Please come home so you can bid me farewell and bury me. Then, God willing, you can return to your army service.

By the way, I have found a girl who would make you a good wife. She is intelligent, and pretty, and she has property. If you like her, perhaps you could get married and stay here for good.

Zhilin thought it over. It's true, he told himself. My mother really isn't well, and I may never get another chance to see her. I'll go home; and if the girl looks good to me, I might get married.

He went to his colonel and got permission to take a furlough. Then he bade goodbye to his fellow officers, treated his men to some four buckets of vodka, and made ready to leave.

A war was going on in the Caucasus at that time, and the roads were not safe for travel. Whenever a Russian went any distance away from a fortress by himself he would be killed by the Tatars. Or else they would take him away with them, high up in the mountains. For this reason there was a standing order that twice a week a military convoy should ride from one fortress to another as protection for travelers. The soldiers formed the advance and rear guard, with the travelers in between.

It was summer. At dawn they made up the wagon train outside the fortress. The convoy detail came out, and they started off. Zhilin was on horseback and his belongings were in one of the wagons.

They had about eighteen miles to go, and the wagon train was moving slowly. Either the soldiers would stop, or a wheel would come off a wagon, or else a horse would balk—and then everybody would have to wait.

By midday, the convoy had covered only half of the distance. It was dusty and hot, with a scorching sun, and there was no shade anywhere: just the barren plain, without even a tree or bush along the road.

Zhilin was riding up ahead. He would stop and wait until the wagon train had caught up with him; then from back in the rear he would hear the bugle blow, giving the signal for another delay. Zhilin asked himself: Wouldn't it be better to go on alone without the soldiers? I have a good horse under me, and even if I do meet up with some Tatars I can get away. But then again, maybe I shouldn't go alone.

He halted to think it over. Another officer, Kostylin, rode up to him. He was carrying a rifle. "Let's go on alone, Zhilin," he said. "I can't take any more of this. I'm getting hungry. And the heat! My shirt is soaking wet!"

Kostylin was in fact stout and heavy-set, and the sweat was pouring off him.

Zhilin thought a moment, and then asked, "Is your rifle loaded?"

"Yes."

"All right then, let's go. But remember, we mustn't get separated."

So they rode on ahead through the steppe, chatting, but at the same time keeping an eye on both sides of the road. In both directions one could see far into the distance.

At the edge of the plain, the road went through a ravine between two hills. Zhilin said, "We'd better ride up to the top of the hill and look around. If we don't, the Tatars might come galloping down from the hill before we've even seen them."

But Kostylin answered, "Why look around? Let's keep going."

Zhilin disagreed. "No," he said. "You stay down here, and I'll go up for a quick look." And he started up the hill to the left.

His horse was a hunter—a mare that he had bought for a hundred rubles when she was still a colt; he had trained her himself. She carried him up the steep hillside as though on wings. Just as he reached the top of the hill he saw, right in front of him and only a short distance away, a band of Tatars on horseback. There were about thirty of them.

As soon as Zhilin saw them he turned back. But they had spotted him too, and set off after him, getting out their guns while at full gallop.

Zhilin raced down the hillside as fast as his horse could go, shouting to Kostylin, "Get your rifle!" And in thought he told his horse, "Get me out of here, old girl! And don't stumble, because if you do it's all over with me. But once I get to that rifle, they'll never capture me."

Kostylin, though, didn't wait for him. Instead, as soon as he saw the Tatars he headed for the next fortress as fast as he could go, whipping his horse first on one flank and then the other. All that could be seen was a cloud of dust and the horse's tail flying out behind.

Zhilin saw that the situation was bad. The rifle was gone, and he couldn't do anything with just his sword. He turned his horse around and headed back toward the convoy, hoping to escape that way. Then he saw a group of six Tatars racing to cut him off. His horse was a good one, but theirs were still better; and besides, they had a favorable angle of interception. He tried to rein in his horse to turn around again, but by this time she was completely out of his control: she went racing straight toward the Tatars. Zhilin saw a red-bearded Tatar on a gray horse coming at him, screaming, his teeth bared, and his rifle at the ready.

I know you devils, Zhilin thought. If you take me alive you'll put me in a pit and lash me with a whip. But you won't get me alive . . . Zhilin was not a big man, but he was courageous. He drew his sword and headed straight for the red-bearded Tatar, thinking, "Either I'll run him down with my horse, or I'll cut him down with my sword."

But when he was just a few feet away, someone shot at him from behind and hit his horse instead. She came crashing to the ground, pinning Zhilin's leg under her.

He tried to get up, but two vile-smelling Tatars were already on top of him, twisting his arms behind his back. He struggled to get loose, and threw off one of the Tatars; but three more of them jumped off their horses and began to club him on the head with their rifle butts. He began to reel; a dimness came to his eyes. The Tatars grabbed hold of him, got spare cinches from their saddles, twisted his arms behind him and tied them with a Tatar knot, then dragged him from his saddle. They knocked off his cap, pulled off his boots, and ransacked everything he had, taking his money and his watch, and tearing his clothes. Zhilin looked over at his horse. She, poor thing, was lying on her side, just as she had fallen, her legs kicking in the air. In her head there was a hole from which dark blood actually spurted out, soaking the dusty ground for several feet around.

One of the Tatars went over to her and tried to take off the saddle. But she continued to kick. He drew his knife and slit her throat. A brief whistling sound came from her windpipe; she quivered, and then died.

The Tatars took the saddle and the trappings. The red-bearded one mounted his horse, and the others put Zhilin on behind him, strapping him to the other man's belt so that he wouldn't fall off. Then they took him up into the mountains.

Zhilin sat behind the Tatar, swaying from side to side, his face bumping against the man's foul-smelling back. All he could see in front of him was the Tatar's burly back, his sinewy neck, and just below his cap, the rear of his head—close-shaven and bluish-looking. Zhilin had a cut on his own head, and the blood was running into his eyes. But he could neither sit up straight on the horse nor wipe the blood from his face. His arms were tied in such a way that they made his collarbone ache.

They rode for a long time through the mountains, forded a river, came out on a road, and went through a little valley. Zhilin wanted to take note of the route they were following; but he couldn't see, and he couldn't turn around.

It began to grow dark. They forded another river and started climbing up a rocky mountain. There was a smell of smoke, and some dogs could be heard barking. They had reached the "*aul*," as the Tatar villages are called.

The Tatars got off their horses. A group of Tatar children assembled, surrounded Zhilin, and, squealing with joy, began to throw stones at him. One of the Tatars drove them away. He took Zhilin off the horse,

and summoned a workman—a *Nogai** with high cheek-
bones who was wearing only a shirt so torn that his
whole chest was exposed. The Tatar gave him an order.
The workman went and got a foot-stock—a pair of oak
blocks with iron rings attached to them, on one of which
was a clamp and a lock.

They untied Zhilin's arms, put the foot-stock on him,
took him to a shed, and pushed him in, locking the door.
He fell on a pile of manure. When he had lain there a
while, he groped around in the dark for a more com-
fortable spot, and then lay down again.

II

That whole night, he scarcely slept. The nights were
short. Seeing daylight through a crack in the wall, he
roused himself, widened the crack, and looked out.

Through the crack he could see a road going down
the mountainside, and on the right a Tatar hut with two
trees growing near it. A black dog was lying in the doorway, and a goat and her kids were moving about, twitch-
ing their tails. Then he saw a young Tatar woman coming up the mountainside. She was wearing a loose-fitting
colored blouse, trousers, and boots; also a caftan with
which she had covered her head. On top of her head was
a big tin water pitcher. As she walked along, her bent
back quivering, she led by the hand a young Tatar boy

* I.e., a member of the Nogai tribe in the Caucasus (Tr.).

with a shaven head who wore only a shirt. She went into the hut with the water. Then out of the hut came the red-bearded Tatar. He wore a quilted silk tunic with a silver-handled dagger in his belt, and slippers on his otherwise-bare feet. On his head was a tall, black sheepskin cap tilted toward the back. He came out of the hut, stretched, and rubbed his hand over his red beard. After standing there a little longer, he gave some orders to the workman and went away.

Then two boys came by on horses that they had just watered, and whose mouths were still wet. More boys came running—they had shaven heads and wore only shirts without trousers. The boys came over to the shed, took a long, dry branch, and shoved it into the crack. Zhilin roared at them so loudly that they squealed and ran away, their bare knees glistening.

Zhilin was thirsty—his throat was parched. If they'd only come in here, he thought. Then he heard the door of the shed being unlocked. The red-bearded Tatar entered, accompanied by another one—a shorter man of swarthy complexion. He had black, gleaming eyes, high color in the cheeks, a neat beard, and a cheerful face. He was better dressed than his companion, in a blue silk tunic trimmed with silver braid, big silver knife in his belt, red morocco leather slippers also trimmed in silver, another pair of heavier slippers over these, and a tall, white sheepskin cap.

The red-bearded Tatar muttered something that

sounded like a curse, and then leaned against the lintel
of the low doorway, toying with his knife and glaring
like a wolf at Zhilin. But the swarthy one—quick and
lively as if there were steel springs in his legs—came
straight over to Zhilin, squatted down, gave him a broad
grin, patted him on the shoulder, and began to jabber
something over and over again in his own language—
winking, clicking his tongue, and constantly repeating
"*korosho urus, korosho urus.*"*

Zhilin didn't understand a word. "Drink," he said.
"Give water—drink."

The swarthy man laughed. "*Korosho urus,*" he repeated, and continued to babble in his own tongue.

Zhilin made signs with his hands and lips to show him
he wanted some water.

The swarthy fellow understood. He laughed, looked
toward the doorway and shouted "Dina!" to someone.

A girl came on the run. She was about thirteen years
old, scrawny, with delicate features, but a facial resem-
blance to the swarthy man. Plainly, she was his daughter. She too had gleaming black eyes. She wore a long,
loose-fitting blue blouse with wide sleeves and no belt. It
had red trimming on the hem, the front, and the sleeves.
She wore trousers and slippers, with a pair of high-
heeled shoes over the slippers, and a necklace made entirely of Russian half-ruble coins. Her head was uncov-
ered, and in her braided black hair she wore a ribbon
* In the Tatar's broken Russian: "Good Russian!"

decorated with flat metal ornaments and a silver one-ruble coin.

Her father gave the girl an order. She ran out and returned with a tin pitcher. She gave Zhilin the water, then squatted down, bending so far over that her shoulders were lower than her knees. She sat there, eyes wide, and stared at Zhilin while he drank, as though he were some kind of wild beast.

Zhilin handed the pitcher back to her, and she bounded away like a wild goat. Even her father had to laugh.

He gave her another order. She took the pitcher, ran out, came back with some unleavened bread on a plate, and again sat down, bent low, and stared at Zhilin without once dropping her eyes.

Then the three of them went out. The door was locked once again.

A short time later the *Nogai* came in and said to Zhilin: "*Aida*, the master, *aida*."

He didn't know any Russian, either. All Zhilin could understand was that he was being ordered to go somewhere.

He followed the *Nogai*, still in the stocks, unable really to walk or direct his feet. He saw a Tatar village —ten houses and their kind of a church, with a minaret. In front of one house stood three horses with saddles on them. Little boys were holding the bridles. The swarthy Tatar bounded out of this particular house, gesturing to Zhilin that he should come in. Laughing, and still talking in his own language, he himself went back inside.

Zhilin entered the house. He found himself in an attractive room, with smooth walls of clay. Featherbeds of various colors were set along the front wall; costly rugs were hung on the side walls; and pistols and swords, all of silver, were mounted on the rugs. To one side was a small stove, on the level of the floor. The latter was earthen, and as clean as a threshing-floor. One of the corners of the room near the entrance was entirely covered in felt; over the felt were rugs, and on the rugs were feather cushions. Sitting on the rugs, and wearing only slippers now, were three Tatars: the swarthy one, the red-bearded one, and another guest. Each of them had a feather cushion behind his back; and before each of them were a plate of pancakes, a bowl of melted butter, and a jug of Tatar beer, called *buza*.

The Tatars were eating with their hands, which were all covered with butter.

The swarthy one jumped to his feet and told the *Nogai* to seat Zhilin off to one side—not on the rug, but on the bare ground. Then he reclined on the rug again, and offered his guests more pancakes and *buza*. The *Nogai* workman seated Zhilin where he had been told to, took off his outer slippers, placed them by the door beside the others, and sat down on the felt near the

masters. He watched them eat, wiping the saliva from his mouth.

When they had eaten the pancakes, a Tatar woman came in, wearing trousers and the same kind of blouse the girl had worn, her head covered with a kerchief. She took away the butter and the pancakes and brought in a handsome wash basin and a narrow-necked jug. The Tatars washed their hands, folded them, got down on their knees, blew in the air on all sides, and said a prayer. Then the third man turned to Zhilin and began speaking to him in Russian. "You were taken prisoner by Kazi-Mohammed," he said, indicating the Tatar with the red beard, "and he has turned you over to Abdul-Murat." He indicated the swarthy man. "Abdul-Murat is now your master."

Zhilin remained silent. Abdul-Murat started talking, then, pointing to Zhilin, began laughing, and repeating *"soldat urus, korosho urus."*

The interpreter said, "He commands you to write a letter home asking for a ransom. As soon as the money comes, he'll set you free."

Zhilin thought a while, and then asked, "Does he want a big ransom?"

The Tatars talked it over briefly, and then the interpreter said, "Three thousand in coins."

"No," Zhilin said, "I can't pay that much."

Abdul jumped to his feet, began waving his arms, and said something to Zhilin—still thinking Zhilin would understand him. The interpreter translated: "How much will you give?"

Zhilin reflected a moment. "Five hundred rubles," he said. At this the Tatars all started jabbering at once. Abdul began to shout at the red-bearded one, talking so excitedly that he spluttered. But the latter merely scowled and made a clicking noise with his tongue.

When they had quieted down, the interpreter said, "Your master thinks five hundred rubles isn't enough ransom. He himself paid two hundred rubles for you. Kazi-Mohammed was in debt to him, and Abdul-Murat took you as payment. Three thousand rubles, or he won't set you free. And if you don't write for it, you'll be put in a pit and whipped."

Zhilin thought, "Eh, with these people, if you act afraid things only get worse." He stood up quickly and said, "And you can tell him, the dog, that if he tries to frighten me I won't give him a single kopek, and I won't write any letter. I've never been afraid of you, and I never will be!"

The interpreter repeated this, and again they all started talking at once.

They jabbered away for a long time. Then the swarthy one jumped to his feet and came over to Zhilin. "*Urus dzhigit,*" he said. "*Dzhigit urus!*" (In their language, *dzhigit* means "a real man.") He laughed again, and said something to the interpreter. The latter translated: "Give him one thousand rubles."

Zhilin stood firm. "Five hundred rubles is all I'll pay. And if you beat me, you won't get anything."

The Tatars conferred together again, then sent the workman out for something. Meantime they kept glancing first at Zhilin, then at the door. The workman came back, bringing with him a heavy-set man, barefooted and in tattered clothes. He too had shackles on his feet.

Zhilin gasped; he had recognized Kostylin. So they had caught him, too!

They sat him down next to Zhilin, and the two of them began to talk while the Tatars watched in silence. Zhilin told what had happened to him. Kostylin said that his horse had balked and his rifle had misfired, and that this very same Abdul had overtaken and captured him.

Abdul leaped to his feet, pointed to Kostylin, and said something. The interpreter translated, saying they both had the same master now, and that the one who gave him money first would be set free first. Then, addressing Zhilin, "Just consider. You go on raging, but your friend is reasonable. He has written home telling them to send five thousand rubles in coins. So he'll be fed well, and won't be punished."

Zhilin said, "My friend can do as he likes. He may be rich, but I'm not. What I said before still goes. I won't write for more than five hundred rubles. Kill me if you want to—but it won't do you any good."

Nobody said anything. Suddenly Abdul jumped up and got a small box from which he took out a pen, a piece of paper, and some ink. He pushed them in front of Zhilin, clapped him on the shoulder, and said, "Write!" He had agreed to the five hundred rubles.

"One more thing," Zhilin said to the interpreter. "Tell him he has to feed us well, give us proper clothing and shoes, and let us stay together—it will be easier on us. Also, he must remove our foot-stocks." Zhilin looked at his master and laughed.

His master laughed back at him, and heard what the interpreter had to say. Then he replied: "I'll give them the very best clothing: a Circassian cloak and boots fine enough for a bridegroom. They'll be fed like princes. And if they want to be together, they can both stay in the shed. But the foot-stocks must not be taken off, or else they'll both escape. Only at night can they be taken off." He sprang to his feet, slapped them on the back, and said: "Yours good, mine good!"

Zhilin wrote the letter, but he put the wrong address on it so that it would never arrive. He was thinking, "I'll escape."

III

They put Zhilin and Kostylin in the shed and brought them corn husks, water in a jug, two old Circassian cloaks, and some worn-out army boots—apparently taken from dead soldiers. When night came the Tatars took off the foot-stocks, but locked the door.

Zhilin and Kostylin lived like this for an entire month. Their master continued to laugh and say, "Yours, Ivan, good; mine, Abdul, good." But they were badly fed— sometimes getting only unleavened bread made from millet flour and baked in the form of flat cakes, or just bread dough.

Kostylin had written home a second time, and was

still waiting for the money to arrive and moping in the meantime. For whole days at a time he would sit there in the shed, counting the hours till the letter arrived. Or else he would sleep.

Zhilin, for his part, knew his letter would never reach home; and he didn't write a second one. He asked himself, "Where would my mother get that much money to ransom me? As it is, she's been living mostly on what I send her. If she had to dig up another five hundred rubles, she'd be ruined financially. No, with God's help I'll get myself out of here on my own."

So he constantly kept on the alert for ways to escape.

He would go through the little mountain village whistling; or else he would sit somewhere making something with his hands—either modeling a doll from clay or weaving some wicker article out of twigs, since he was very skillful at handicrafts.

Once he modeled a clay doll complete with nose, hands and feet, with a Tatar-style blouse besides, and set it on the roof.

Some Tatar women came by for water. Dina, the master's daughter, saw the doll and called the others over to look at it. They put down their water pitchers, looked at the doll, and laughed. Zhilin took it down to give it to them. They laughed again, but were afraid to take it. He put it back, went into the shed, and waited to see what would happen.

Dina ran up, looked around her, snatched up the doll, and ran off.

The next morning, at dawn, Zhilin saw Dina come out to the door stoop with the doll. She had already dressed it in bits of red cloth and was rocking it like a baby, singing a Tatar lullaby. Her mother came out, scolded her, snatched the doll away and broke it, and sent Dina off to work.

Zhilin made another doll, an even better one, and gave it to Dina.

Then one day Dina came in to him with a pitcher. She put it on the ground, sat down and looked at him, laughing, pointing to the pitcher.

"What's she so delighted about?" Zhilin wondered. He picked up the pitcher and began to drink. He had expected water, but it was milk. He drank all of it. "That's good!" he said.

How pleased she was! "Good, Ivan, good!"—and she leapt up, clapped her hands, quickly retrieved the pitcher, and ran out.

From then on she secretly brought him milk every day. And if the Tatars chanced to make cheesecakes and leave them on their roofs to dry, she would bring him some of the cakes when no one was watching. Once, when the master had butchered a ram, she brought him a piece of mutton hidden in her sleeve. She threw it in to him and then ran away.

One day there was a big storm, and for a whole hour the rain poured down as though from buckets. All of the streams became turbid. In places where there had been fords, the water now rushed along, seven feet deep,

carrying big stones with it. Rivulets were running everywhere, and a roaring sound echoed through the mountains. When the storm had passed, there were rivulets
still flowing everywhere in the village.

Zhilin asked his master for a knife. With it, he whit-
tled out a shaft and some paddles. He attached the
paddles to a wheel, and hooked up two dolls to the ends
of the shaft.

Some of the village girls brought him scraps of cloth,
and he dressed the dolls—one as a man, the other as a
woman. He made sure they were well fastened, and
then lowered the wheel into a stream. The wheel turned,
and the dolls danced.

Everybody in the village came to see: boys, girls,
women, men. They clacked their tongues. "*Ai, urus! Ai,
Ivan!*" they cried.

Once, when Abdul's Russian watch got broken, the
Tatar called Zhilin over and showed it to him, shaking
his head. Zhilin said, "Give it to me. I'll fix it."

He took the watch, worked at it with his little knife,
and got it apart. Then he put it back together again and
returned it. The watch ran.

The master was overjoyed. He brought Zhilin an old,
tattered tunic of his as a gift. Zhilin couldn't very well
refuse it; and besides, he could use it as a cover at night.

From that time on Zhilin grew famous as a master
craftsman. People began coming to him from distant
villages—some bringing watches to be fixed, others rifles

or pistols. His master gave him some tools: a pair of tweezers, a gimlet, and a file.

On one occasion, when a Tatar was sick, some of the others came to him and said, "Go and cure him." Zhilin didn't know anything at all about medical treatment. But he went, took a look at the man, and said to himself, "Maybe he'll get well on his own." He went back to his shed, got some water and sand, and mixed them together. With the Tatars looking on, he whispered a few words over the water, and then gave it to the man to drink. Luckily for him, the man got well.

Zhilin began to understand a little of their language. And some of the Tatars came to like him. When they wanted him they would call out "Ivan! Ivan!" But others still looked at him askance, as if he were a wild animal.

The Tatar with the red beard didn't like Zhilin. Whenever he saw him he would frown and turn away, or else he would curse him.

Then there was the old man who lived outside the village, a little way down the mountainside. The only time Zhilin saw the old man was when he came to the mosque to pray. He was short, and wore a white towel wrapped around his cap. His beard and mustache were neatly trimmed and as white as down; his wrinkled face was as red as brick. His nose was hooked like a hawk's beak, his eyes were gray and evil-looking, and he had no teeth except two canines. He would walk along with a crutch, wearing a turban on his head, and glare around him like a wolf. The moment he saw Zhilin he would give a snort and turn away.

Once Zhilin went down the mountainside to see where the old man lived. Coming along the path, he saw a little orchard with a stone fence around it. Behind the fence were fruit trees—sweet cherry, peach, and apricot—and a hut with a flat roof. When he was closer he could see some beehives woven from straw, with bees flying and buzzing around them. The old man was there, down on his knees, fussing with the beehives. Zhilin stretched higher to see better, and his foot-stocks clanked. The old man looked around, gave a shrill yell, pulled a pistol from his belt, and fired. Zhilin barely had time to duck down behind the fence.

The old man came to Zhilin's master and complained. Abdul summoned Zhilin and asked him, with a laugh, "Why did you go to the old man's place?"

"I didn't do anything to harm him," Zhilin said. "I just wanted to see how he lived."

Abdul explained this to the old man, but he just raged, hissed, and muttered something—baring his canine teeth and shaking his fists at Zhilin.

Zhilin didn't understand all of it, but he gathered that the old man had told Abdul to kill the Russians instead of keeping them in the village.

The old man left. Zhilin asked who he was. "He is a great man," Abdul said. "He was the bravest among us.

He killed many Russians, and was rich. He had three wives and eight sons. They all lived together in one village. Then the Russians came and destroyed the village, and they killed seven of his sons. Only one son was left alive, and he surrendered to the Russians. The old man went to the Russians and surrendered, too. He lived among them for three months, found his son, killed him, and escaped. Then and there, he gave up fighting. He went to Mecca to pray—and that's why he wears a turban. Anyone who has been to Mecca is called a *Hadji* and wears a turban. The old man is very much against you Russians. He told me to kill you, but that's something I can't do. I paid good money for you; and besides, I've come to like you, Ivan. It's not just that I wouldn't kill you; if I hadn't given my word I wouldn't even let you go." He laughed, and said in his broken Russian: "Yours, Ivan, good; mine, Abdul, good."

IV

Such was Zhilin's life for a whole month. In the daytime he went here and there in the village, or worked at some handicraft; at nightfall, when the village became quiet, he dug in his shed. The digging was difficult because of the rock; but he cut through it with his file and dug a tunnel under the wall that he could crawl through when the time came. He thought, "If only I could get to know this area, so I'd know which way to go. But the Tatars won't tell me a single thing."

Once, when his master was away, he left the village after dinner and went higher up the mountain; he wanted to get a look at the area from up there. But Abdul had ordered his son to follow Zhilin and not let him out of his sight. Now the boy came running after him, shouting, "Don't go away! My father said you mustn't. I'll call the people in the village!"

Zhilin began to reassure him. "I'm not going far," he said. "I'm just going up this mountainside to get some herbs that I need for treating your people. Come along with me. With these foot-stocks on, I can't escape anyway. And tomorrow I'll make you a bow and some arrows."

The boy was convinced, and came along. Just looking at it, the ridge didn't seem much of a climb; but with shackled feet it was hard going. Zhilin kept on and on; and finally, with great effort, he reached the top. He sat down and began to survey the area. To the south of a shed there was a valley where a herd of horses was grazing; and at the lower end of the valley another Tatar village could be seen. Beyond the village there was another ridge, even steeper; and beyond that, still another. Between them were blue growths of forest; still farther were more ridges, rising higher and higher. And highest of all were the snow-capped mountains, white as sugar. One of them, even loftier than the others, stood up sharply like a sword. To both east and west there was nothing but mountains and, in the valleys, Tatar villages from which smoke was rising.

Well, Zhilin thought, all that country is theirs. Then he began to survey the Russian side. Just below him he saw a stream and the village of his captivity, with orchards around it. Some village women were sitting at the stream's edge, washing clothes; they looked like tiny dolls. Beyond the village there was a lower ridge, and then two more mountains covered with forest growth. Between them was a bluish stretch of flat land; and far in the distance, above the flatlands, a cloud of smoke was drifting. Zhilin tried to remember where the sun had risen and set when he was living in the fortress. Then it came to him that the fortress must be right there in the valley. That was the way he should go when he escaped—between those two mountains.

The sun began to go down. The snow-capped peaks went from white to scarlet; the dark ridges grew even darker; mist rose from the gorges; the valley where the Russian fortress was supposed to be blazed red in the sunset. Zhilin strained to see, and caught a glimpse of something hovering there in the valley—smoke from a chimney, perhaps. He had the notion that this, too, came from the Russian fortress.

It was already late. They could hear the call of the mullah. The herd was being brought in, and the cattle were lowing. The boy kept calling "Let's go!" But Zhilin didn't want to leave.

Finally they returned to the village. "Well," Zhilin thought, "now I know the area; it's time to escape." He would have liked to make a run for it that same night. The moon was on the wane and the nights were dark now. But unfortunately the Tatar men had come back that evening. Usually, when they returned to the village, they brought livestock with them and were in good spirits. But this time they weren't herding livestock. Instead, they brought back a Tatar, dead in his saddle; he was the brother of the red-bearded man, Kazi-Mohammed.

The men were in a wrathful mood as they entered the village. Everyone gathered for the burial; and Zhilin, too, went out to watch. They wrapped the corpse in a sheet, not using any coffin, carried it outside the village to a sycamore grove, and set it down on the grass. The mullah came, and the elders gathered, towels wrapped around their caps. They took off their shoes and squatted before the corpse, the mullah in front, behind him a row of three elders in turbans, and behind them still more Tatars.

They sat there in silence, their eyes downcast. They were silent for a long time. Then the mullah raised his head and said: "Allah!" (meaning 'God'). He uttered just that one word, and then they all lowered their eyes again and were silent for another long time. They sat absolutely still.

Once again the mullah raised his head: "Allah!"

"Allah!" they murmured in response, and then fell silent once more. The body was lying there on the grass, and they sat there as immobile as the corpse. Not one of them stirred. The only sound was the rustling of the leaves in the sycamores.

Then the mullah read a prayer, after which they all rose, picked up the body, and carried it away in their arms. They took it to a pit which had not been dug straight down in the usual way, but hollowed out under the ground—like a vault. They grasped the dead man by his armpits and ankles, jackknifed him, lowered him gently, pushed him under the ground without disturbing his position, and then folded his hands on his lap.

The *Nogai* brought some green bulrushes, which they laid in the pit. Then they quickly filled it with earth, leveled the top, and set a stone upright at the head of the grave. They trampled down the earth, and sat down again in a row before the grave. They were silent for a long time.

"Allah! Allah! Allah!" They sighed and got up.

The red-bearded man, Kazi-Mohammed, distributed some money among the elders. Then he got up, took a whip, lashed himself three times on the forehead, and went home.

The next morning Zhilin saw Kazi-Mohammed, followed by three other Tatars, leading a mare out of the
village. When they were a distance away Kazi-Mohammed took off his tunic, rolled his sleeves up on his
brawny arms, drew a dagger, and sharpened it on a
whetstone. The other Tatars pulled the mare's head
back, and Kazi-Mohammed came over and slit her
throat, threw her to the ground, and began to flay her
—ripping the hide off with his hands.

The women and girls came, and began washing the
entrails and innards. Then they cut the mare up into
pieces and carried them back to the hut. Everyone in
the village assembled at Kazi-Mohammed's home for
the funeral feast.

For three days they ate mare's meat and drank *buza*
in memory of the deceased. All of the Tatar men were
on hand. On the fourth day at dinner time Zhilin noticed they were getting ready to go somewhere. The
horses were led out, and when all was ready about ten
men, including Kazi-Mohammed, rode off. Only Abdul
remained at home.

V

The moon was new, and the nights were still dark.
"Well," Zhilin thought, "this is the time to escape." And
he said so to Kostylin. But Kostylin was afraid.

"How could we escape? We don't even know which
way to go."

"I know the way."

"But we can't get there in just one night."

"If we don't get through we'll spend the night in the forest. I have some flatcakes we can eat.

"Well, are you just going to stay here?" said Zhilin. "If they send the money, fine; but they may not get that much money together. Besides, the Tatars are angry now because the Russians killed one of their men; they're talking about killing you and me."

Kostylin pondered and pondered. Then he said, "All right, let's go."

Zhilin crawled into the tunnel and dug it out a little wider so that Kostylin could get through. Then they sat and waited until everything was quiet outside.

As soon as the villagers had settled down, Zhilin crawled under the wall and came out above ground. He whispered to Kostylin: "Come on!" Kostylin crawled through; but on the way he jarred a rock with his foot, and it made a ringing sound.

Abdul had a vicious-tempered watchdog—a motley-colored one called Ulyashin. Zhilin had fed the dog several times. Now he heard him start to bark as he ran toward them, and some other dogs joined in the chorus. Zhilin whistled softly and tossed the dog a flatcake. Ulyashin recognized him, wagged his tail, and stopped barking.

Abdul had heard the barking, and shouted from his hut: "*Gayt, gayt, Ulyashin!*"

But Zhilin scratched the dog behind his ears, and he kept quiet, rubbing against Zhilin's legs and wagging his tail.

They crouched behind a corner of the building. Everything was still, except for the coughing sounds made by the sheep in their pen, and the water purling over the rocks in the ravine. It was dark; the stars stood high in the sky; over the mountain the young moon glowed red, the horns of the crescent pointing upward as it descended. The valleys were filled with mist as white as milk.

Zhilin stood up. "Come on," he said.

They started off. But just as they did, they heard the call of the mullah from his rooftop: "*Allah, Besmillah! Ilrakhman!*" That meant for the people to go to the mosque.

They crouched down again, hugging the wall, and stayed there until the villagers had passed by. Once again it became quiet.

"Well, with God's help!" They crossed themselves and set off. They went through the yard and down the slope to the stream, crossed the stream, and went along the ravine. There was a heavy mist in the ravine, but overhead the stars shone brightly. Zhilin could tell by the stars what direction they were taking. The mist was pleasantly cool, and the going was easy, except for their awkward boots, worn down at the heels. Zhilin took his off and threw them away. Barefoot, he leaped from rock to rock, looking up at the stars every now and then. Kostylin began to lag behind.

"Go a little slower," he said. "These damned boots have given me blisters."

"Then take them off; it's easier that way."

Kostylin went barefoot, too, but that was even worse: he cut his feet on the rocks and lagged farther behind.

Zhilin said, "If you cut your feet, they'll heal. But if they catch up with us, they'll kill us. And that'll be worse." Kostylin didn't answer; he just followed along uttering little moans.

They traveled the bottom of the ravine for a long time. Then, to the right, they heard dogs barking. Zhilin stopped and looked around. Groping his way, he climbed up the side of the ravine. "Oh, oh," he said, "we made a mistake going to the right. There's one of their villages here. I saw it from the mountain. We have to go back and then go left up the mountainside into the forest."

"Let's stop for a while and rest," Kostylin said. "My feet are bleeding all over."

"Don't worry, they'll get better. Try to be lighter on your feet when you jump—like this." Whereupon Zhilin ran back and then to the left, up the mountainside toward the forest.

Kostylin still lagged behind, groaning. Zhilin told him to keep quiet and went on ahead.

They went up the mountainside. They plunged into

the woods, and what clothing they had left was torn to shreds. Then they came upon a path through the woods, and started following it.

"Stop!" There was the sound of hoofbeats along the path. They stood still and listened. There were more hoofbeats, like those of a horse; then they ceased. The men started off again, and again they heard hoofbeats. They stopped and the hoofbeats stopped, too. Zhilin crept closer. In the clear area along the path he saw something that looked like a horse but was not a horse, and on top of it something weird-looking that did not resemble a man. Then he heard it snort. "What the devil?" Zhilin whistled softly, and it shuffled off the path and went crashing through the forest like a storm, breaking branches as it went.

Kostylin almost fainted with fright. But Zhilin laughed. "It's a stag," he said. "Just listen to the way his antlers crash through the forest. We're afraid of him, and he's afraid of us."

They went on. The constellation of Ursa Major had already begun to drop down in the sky, and it wouldn't be long until morning. They had no idea whether they were going in the right direction or not. Zhilin was pretty sure that this was the same path along which the Tatars had taken him, and that they had only about seven miles to go before reaching the Russians. But there was nothing really certain to go by, and at night it was hard for them to tell just where they were.

They came into a clearing. Kostylin sat down and said: "You can do as you like, but I'm not going any farther. My feet have given out."

Zhilin tried to persuade him.

"No," he answered, "I'm not going on. I can't."

Zhilin lost his temper; he spat and swore at Kostylin. "All right then. I'll go on alone. Goodbye!"

Kostylin jumped up and came along. They walked another three miles or so. The mist in the forest became even thicker; they couldn't see a thing in front of them, and the stars were scarcely visible.

Suddenly, from up ahead of them, they heard the sound of a horse trotting, his hoofs striking stones in the path. Zhilin dropped flat on his belly, and put his ear to the ground. "No doubt about it," he said. "There's a horse coming our way."

They scrambled into the underbrush, and waited. Zhilin crawled nearer to the path again and looked. A Tatar, on horseback, was driving a cow along, humming a tune. He passed by, and Zhilin went back to Kostylin. "Well, God brought us through that one. Come on, let's go."

Kostylin tried to get up, but fell back. "God help me, I just can't do it. My strength is gone."

He was a heavy, pudgy man. He had begun to sweat, and then been chilled by the mist in the forest—besides which his feet were badly cut up. He just came apart at the seams.

Zhilin tried to help him up, but he cried out, "Oy, it hurts!"

Zhilin's heart sank. "Must you shout? Don't forget there's a Tatar somewhere near. He might hear you." Meanwhile, Zhilin was thinking, "He's really done in. What am I going to do with him? I can't just abandon a comrade."

"Come on," he said. "Get up and climb on my back. If you can't walk any more, I'll carry you." He got Kostylin up on his back, held him under the thighs, and went down the path lugging him. "For the love of God," he said, "quit strangling me! Hang onto my shoulders instead of my neck."

It was very hard going for Zhilin. He himself was exhausted and his feet were bleeding. He would bend lower, or straighten up, or hoist Kostylin up higher on his back as he lugged him along the path.

Apparently the Tatar had heard Kostylin cry out, because Zhilin heard someone behind them on horseback, shouting in their language. Zhilin ducked into the underbrush. The Tatar grabbed his rifle and took a shot, but missed. Then he gave a yell in Tatar, and galloped away down the path.

"Well, friend, we're done for," Zhilin said. "Now that dog will get the other Tatars together and they'll come after us. If we don't make another two miles before they catch up, we're finished." And, thinking of Kostylin, he said to himself, "It was the devil's doing

that I brought this ball-and-chain along with me. Without him I could have got away long ago."

Kostylin said, "Go on alone. Why should you get
caught because of me?"

"No, I can't do that. It's not right to abandon a comrade."

Zhilin got him up across his shoulders in a fireman's
carry, and they went for almost another mile in this
way. There was nothing but forest all the way, with no
end of it in sight. The mist had begun to break up—
it was as though little clouds had descended to ground
level—and the stars were no longer visible. Zhilin was
utterly exhausted.

They came to a spring, lined with stones, beside the
path. They stopped, and Zhilin put Kostylin down.
"Let's rest a bit," he said, "and get a drink. And we can
eat the flatcakes. It can't be far now."

He had just started to drink when he heard hoofbeats
from behind. Once again they threw themselves into
the underbrush, rolled down the slope, and lay there.

They heard Tatar voices. The Tatars had stopped in
exactly the same spot where they had left the path.
They heard them talk briefly together, then sick a dog
after them. There was a crashing sound in the bushes,
and then the dog—one they had never seen before—
came straight at them. It stopped and began to bark.

After it, crawling through the underbrush, came the
Tatars, who were likewise strangers. They seized Zhilin

and Kostylin, bound them, sat them on horses, and took them away.

When they had gone about two miles they met Abdul and two other Tatars. Abdul exchanged a few words with the captors, then put the Russians on two of his own horses and took them back to the village.

For once, Abdul was not laughing; and he didn't say a word to them.

They reached the village at dawn. Zhilin and Kostylin were set down in the street. The children came running, and attacked them with stones and whips, screeching.

The Tatars gathered together in a little circle, and the old man from down the mountainside joined them. They began to talk among themselves. Zhilin understood that they were deciding what to do with Kostylin and himself. Some of them said the Russians should be taken higher up into the mountains, while the old man said they should be killed. Abdul argued with him, saying, "I paid money for them, and I'm going to get a ransom for them." But the old man said, "They won't pay you anything; you'll get only trouble from them. Anyway, it's a sin to feed Russians. Kill them and be done with it."

They broke up. Abdul came over to Zhilin. "If I don't get your ransom in two weeks," he said, "I'll give you a real flogging. And if you try to escape again, I'll kill you like a dog. Now write another letter, and see that you do it right."

He brought paper, and they both wrote letters. Then

foot-stocks were put on them, and they were taken behind the mosque to where there was a pit about twelve
feet deep. The two of them were put into the pit.

VI

Life became very hard to bear. Their foot-stocks
were never removed, and they were never allowed out
of the pit. Bread dough was thrown down to them as
though they were dogs, and they got their water from
a pitcher lowered into the pit. The pit was foul-smelling,
stifling, and damp. Kostylin became seriously ill; his
body swelled, and he ached all over with rheumatism.
He groaned constantly, except when he slept.

Zhilin, too, was despondent. He could see that the
situation was very bad; and he didn't know how to get
out of it. He began digging a tunnel, but there was no
place to put the dirt: his master saw it, and threatened
to kill him.

One day when he was squatting there in the pit,
dreaming of a free life and moping, a flatcake suddenly
fell into his lap, followed by another, and then a hail of
cherries. He looked up, and there was Dina. She looked
down at him, laughed, and ran away. Immediately
Zhilin wondered, "Couldn't Dina help?"

He cleared out a little corner of the pit, dug up some
clay, and began to model miniature figures. He made
dolls, horses, and dogs. When she comes, he thought,
I'll throw them up to her.

But the next day Dina didn't come right away. Listening, Zhilin heard instead the sound of hoofbeats as several riders went by. The Tatars gathered at the mosque. They were arguing, shouting, and talking about the Russians. Zhilin could hear the old man's voice. He didn't make it all out, but he gathered that the Russian troops were nearby. The Tatars were afraid they would enter the village, and they didn't know what to do with the prisoners.

They talked together some more, and then split up. Suddenly Zhilin heard a rustling sound overhead. He looked up and saw Dina squatting on the edge of the pit, her head down between her knees. She was leaning so far over that her necklace dangled over the pit and her eyes were shining like stars. She pulled two cheese-cakes out from under her sleeve and threw them down. Zhilin took them and said, "Why have you stayed away so long? I've made some toys for you—here!" And he began to toss them up to her, one at a time.

But Dina shook her head and wouldn't look at them. "Don't do that," she said.

She sat there in silence for a while, and then she said, "Ivan, they want to kill you." And she pointed at her own neck.

"Who wants to kill me?"

"My father; the elders told him to. But I feel sorry for you."

"If you feel sorry for me," he said, "you should bring me a long pole."

She shook her head to tell him it was impossible. He clasped his hands and pleaded with her. "Please, Dina! Bring it, Dinushka!"

"I can't," she said. "They're all here now——they'd see me." And she went away.

That evening Zhilin was sitting there wondering what would happen. He kept looking up above him. The stars were out, but the moon hadn't risen yet. The mullah called, and then everything was still. Zhilin began to doze off, thinking, "The girl will be afraid to do anything."

Suddenly some pellets of clay rained down on his head. He looked up and saw a long pole sticking out over the edge of the pit. Then it began to dip and come down.

Zhilin was overjoyed. He grabbed the pole and pulled it down to him: it was a strong one. He had seen it once before on the roof of his master's house.

He looked up; high in the sky the stars were shining brightly, and just over the edge of the pit Dina's eyes were gleaming in the darkness like the eyes of a cat.

She leaned down over the edge of the pit and whispered, "Ivan! Ivan!" waving her hand in front of her face as a sign that he should speak softly.

"What?" Zhilin asked.

"They've all left. Only two of them are here now."

"Well, Kostylin," he said to his companion, "let's go. We'll make one last try. I'll carry you."

Kostylin wouldn't even consider it. "No," he said, "I'll never get out of here. How could I walk, when I don't even have the strength to turn around?"

"All right, then. Goodbye—don't think ill of me." And the two men embraced.

Zhilin grasped the pole, told Dina to hold it steady, and started climbing up. He slipped back a couple of times, because the foot-stocks hindered him. But Kostylin supported his friend from below, and somehow he managed to make it to the top. Dina grabbed hold of his shirt with her little hands, pulling as hard as she could, and laughing.

Zhilin pulled the pole up and said, "Put it back where it belongs, Dina. Otherwise, they'll find it's gone, and give you a beating." She went off with the pole, and Zhilin started down the mountainside. When he had reached the bottom of a steep slope he took a sharp-edged rock and tried to break the lock off the foot-stocks. But it was a strong one that wouldn't break, and besides the method was clumsy.

He heard someone running down the slope, skipping lightly along, and thought, "That must be Dina again."

She ran up to him, took the rock, and said, "Let me try."

She got down on her knees and began working at it; but her hands were as slender as twigs, and had no strength. She dropped the rock and began to cry.

Zhilin started working at it again, and she squatted

down, one hand on his shoulder. He looked around and saw a reddish glow above the mountain; the moon was rising. He told himself that he'd have to get through the ravine and into the forest before the moonlight became bright.

He stood up and threw the rock away. Even with the foot-stocks still on, he had to get moving. "Goodbye, Dinushka," he said. "I'll remember you all my life."

She took hold of him and ran her hands over his body, trying to find a place to put the flatcakes she had brought. He took them from her. "Thank you, my clever one," he said. "Who will make dolls for you when I'm gone?" And he stroked her head.

Dina started to cry, covered her face with her hands, and ran up the mountainside, leaping like a young goat. There was no other sound in the darkness but the clinking of the coins in the long braid down her back.

Zhilin crossed himself, picked up the lock of the foot-stocks and held it so it wouldn't make a clinking noise, and started off, dragging one foot behind the other and keeping an eye on the glow in the sky where the moon would come up. He knew the way; there were about five miles to go straight ahead. The main thing was to reach the forest in time.

He crossed the stream. Above the mountain, the sky was already brightening. He went along the bottom of the ravine, constantly looking up; the moon wasn't out yet, but the glow was now very bright, and along one side of the ravine the light was becoming clearer and clearer. The night shadows crept down the mountain-side, coming ever nearer to him.

He kept on, staying within the shadows. He hurried, but the moon rose even faster. The mountain peaks to the right were already light. As he was nearing the forest, the moon emerged from behind the mountain, white, clear, bright as day. Every leaf on the trees was visible. On the mountains, all was stillness and clear light, as though in death. The only sound was the purling of the stream below.

Zhilin reached the forest without encountering anybody. Finding a dark place in the woods, he sat down to rest.

He relaxed and ate one of the flatcakes. He got a stone and tried once again to break the lock, but he smashed his hands, not the lock. Then he got up and went along the path. After something less than a mile, he was exhausted and his legs gave out. He dragged on for another ten steps, and then stopped. There's nothing else I can do, he thought. I'll just have to keep going as long as I have any strength left, because once I sit down I'll never get up again. I won't make it to the fortress. So when dawn comes I'll lie low somewhere in the forest, stay there all day, and then set out again when night falls.

He kept going all that night. He encountered two Tatars on horseback, but he heard them coming from a long way off, and hid behind a tree.

The moon had already begun to pale, dew was falling,

and dawn was near. But Zhilin had not yet reached the edge of the forest. "Well," he thought, "I'll go another thirty paces and then head into the woods and sit down." He covered the distance and found that he had almost reached the edge of the forest.

He emerged from the forest into broad daylight. Spread out before him were the plain and the fortress; to the left, at the foot of the slope, campfires were blazing up or dying down, the smoke was curling upward from them, and men were standing around warming themselves.

As he watched, he saw the gleam of rifles; these were Cossacks and soldiers.

Zhilin was beside himself with joy. He gathered the last of his strength and started down the slope. "God forbid," he thought, "that some Tatar on horseback should see me here in the open field! To get so close, and then not to make it!"

The thought had hardly crossed his mind when three Tatars appeared to the left. They saw him and took chase. Zhilin's heart sank. He started waving his arms and shouting with all his might. "Brothers! Help! Brothers!"

The Russians heard him. The mounted Cossacks spurred their horses and started toward him, trying to cut off the Tatars. But they were far away, while the Tatars were close. With his last mite of strength, and hardly knowing what he was doing, Zhilin grabbed up

his foot-stocks and ran toward the Cossacks, crossing himself and shouting "Brothers! Brothers! Brothers!"

There were about fifteen Cossacks. The Tatars took fright and reined up before reaching Zhilin. He ran to meet the Cossacks.

They ringed him, and asked who he was and where he had come from. But Zhilin was so overcome with joy and relief he just wept and kept repeating, "Brothers! Brothers!"

Some of the regular soldiers came crowding around. They gave Zhilin bread and vodka, threw a coat over his shoulders, and broke off the foot-stocks.

The officers recognized him, and he was taken to the fortress. His soldiers were delighted to see him, and his comrades gathered in his room.

He told them everything that had happened to him, and then he said, "So that's how I went home and got married! Seriously, I can see now that I never will get married. It's just not in the cards for me."

And so he remained in service in the Caucasus. As for Kostylin, it was another month before his ransom of five thousand rubles was paid and he was brought back—more dead than alive.

*Emelyan
and the Empty
Drum*

*E*melyan lived at his master's, along with the other workingmen. One day as he was walking across the meadow to work, a frog hopped out in front of him, and he almost squashed it. But he stepped over it and went on. Suddenly he heard someone calling him from behind. He looked back and saw a beautiful maiden standing there. "Emelyan," she asked him, "why don't you get married?"

"How can I get married, pretty maid? All that I am and have you see before you. Nobody would marry me."

"Take me for a wife," she said.

Emelyan immediately fell in love with the maiden. "I'd be very glad to," he said. "But where would we live?"

"That's nothing to worry about," she said. "All you have to do is work a little more and sleep a little less, and we'll be fed and clothed wherever we are."

"Well, all right then," he agreed; "let's get married. But where shall we go?"

"Let's go into the city."

Emelyan and the maiden went to the city. She took him to a little house on the edge of town. They were married and began living there.

One day the Tsar was driving out toward the country. He drove past Emelyan's house, and Emelyan's wife came out to have a look at the Tsar. When he saw her, he was astonished. "Where did that beautiful girl come from?" he wondered.

He stopped his carriage, called Emelyan's wife over, and began to question her.

"Who are you?" he asked.

"The wife of Emelyan, the peasant," she said.

"But why did such a beauty as you marry a peasant? You should be the wife of a tsar."

"Thank you," she said, "for your kind words. But I like being married to a peasant."

The Tsar talked with her a little while longer, and then drove on, returning to his palace. But he couldn't get Emelyan's wife out of his mind. All that night long he couldn't sleep: he kept trying to think of some way to get Emelyan's wife away from him. But he couldn't figure out how to do it. So he sent for his retainers and told them to think up something.

They said to him, "Have Emelyan brought here to the palace as one of the laborers. We'll work him to death, and when his wife is a widow you can take her for yourself."

The Tsar did what they said. He sent for Emelyan to come to work as a helper around the palace, and to bring his wife so she could live there with him.

The messengers came and told Emelyan. His wife said to him, "Go ahead and do it. Work there during the day, and then come back to me at night."

Emelyan went. When he got to the palace, the Tsar's

steward asked him, "Why did you come alone, without your wife?"

"Why should I bring her?" Emelyan said. "She has a home."

They gave Emelyan enough work around the palace grounds for two men. He started in with no hope of getting it all done. But lo and behold! Before evening it was all done. The steward saw that he had finished it, and gave him four times as much for the next day.

Emelyan went home. When he got there he found the house had been swept and picked up, a fire had been made in the stove, and everything was baked and cooked. His wife was sitting at her loom, weaving, waiting for her husband. She greeted him, laid the table for supper, gave him food and drink, and then began to ask him about his work.

"Well," he said, "things are bad. They give me more than I can do. They are wearing me out with work."

"You mustn't give it a thought," she said. "Don't look back to see how much you've done and don't look ahead to see how much you still have to do. Just work, and everything will be finished on time."

Emelyan went to bed. In the morning he went off to work again. He started in working, and not once did he look back. Before he knew it the day was over and the job was finished. It was not yet dark when he went home for the night.

They gave Emelyan more and more work to do; but

he always finished it on time and went home for the night.

A week went by, and the Tsar's retainers saw that they could not wear the peasant out with hard work. So they began to assign him jobs requiring a good deal of skill. But they couldn't get the better of him even in this way. No matter what kind of work they gave him—carpentry, masonry, or roofing work—he always finished it on time and then went home to his wife for the night.

When another week had gone by, the Tsar sent for his retainers and said to them, "Am I feeding you for nothing? Two weeks have gone by, and you have produced no results. You were going to wear him out with work. But every day, from my window, I see him going home singing a song. Are you trying to make fun of me?"

His retainers started to make excuses for themselves. "First," one of them said, "we tried to exhaust him with hard work but nothing was too much for him. He did every job as though it was sweeping up with a broom. And he never got tired. Then we started giving him work that calls for much skill, thinking he wouldn't be clever enough for it. But that didn't succeed, either. It's like some kind of magic. He manages everything; he can do anything. There are no two ways about it: either he is a wizard or his wife is a witch.

"He is the one that's wearing *us* out. Now we want

to give him a job that he can't possibly do. And we have thought up the idea of ordering him to build a cathedral in one day. Send for him, and command him to build an entire cathedral, facing the palace, in one day. And if he doesn't do it, you can have his head cut off for disobeying you."

The Tsar sent for Emelyan. "I hereby command you," he said, "to build me a new cathedral on the square across from the palace. I want it completed by tomorrow evening. If you succeed, I will reward you. If you don't, you will be put to death."

When the Tsar had finished speaking, Emelyan turned around and went home. "Now my end has surely come," he thought.

When he got home, he said to his wife, "You'd better make ready. We must flee from here. It doesn't matter where we go. But if we stay here, we're lost."

"What?" she asked. "Are you so frightened, you want to run away?"

"Why shouldn't I be frightened? The Tsar ordered me to build a cathedral in one day. If I don't build it, he threatens to cut off my head. There's only one thing we can do—run away while we still have time."

His wife did not agree. "The Tsar has many soldiers," she said. "Wherever we go, they will find us. You can't escape him. As long as you have strength left, you must obey."

"But how can I obey when it's more than I can do?"

"Come now, my dear. Don't be downhearted! Eat

your supper and go to bed. In the morning just get up a little earlier, and everything will be finished on time."

Emelyan went to bed. The next morning his wife woke him up. "Run along," she said, "and finish the cathedral quickly. Here is a hammer and nails. There's a day's work left for you."

Emelyan went into the city. Sure enough, when he arrived he saw a new cathedral standing in the square. Just a little work remained to be done. Emelyan began putting on the finishing touches. By evening it was completed.

The Tsar awoke and looked out of the palace window. He saw the cathedral and he saw Emelyan walking around, driving in a nail here and there. But the Tsar was not glad to have the cathedral. Instead, he was vexed that there was no reason for putting Emelyan to death and taking his wife.

Again the Tsar summoned his retainers. "Emelyan has accomplished this task, too," he said, "and I have no grounds for putting him to death. Even this task was not too much for him! You must think up something better. Use your wits well, or I'll execute you before I do him."

This time the counselors came up with the idea that the Tsar should command Emelyan to make a river that would flow around the palace, with ships sailing on it. The Tsar summoned Emelyan and ordered him to perform the new task "If you can build a cathedral in one night," he said, "you can do this bit of work,

too. See that my command is carried out completely by tomorrow. If it is not, I will cut off your head."

Emelyan was even more downhearted than before, and he went home to his wife in a gloomy state of mind.

"Why are you so downhearted?" she asked him. "Has the Tsar given you still another task?"

Emelyan told her what had happened. "We must run away," he said.

But his wife answered, "We can't escape his soldiers; they will find us wherever we go. You must obey."

"But how can I obey?"

"Come now, my dear," she said. "There is no reason to despair. Eat your supper and go to bed. In the morning get up a little earlier than usual, and everything will be finished on time."

Emelyan went to bed. In the morning his wife woke him up. "Go to the palace," she said. "Everything is ready, except for one thing. At the landing opposite the palace there is a little mound of earth. Take a spade and level it off."

Emelyan left. When he reached the city, he saw that there was a river around the palace, with ships sailing on it. He went to the landing across from the palace, found the uneven place, and began to level it off.

The Tsar awakened and saw a river where there had been none before. He saw ships sailing on the river. And he saw Emelyan leveling the little mound of earth with a spade.

The Tsar was furious. He was not pleased with the river or the ships. Instead, he was vexed that he could not put Emelyan to death.

He said to himself, "There is no task that he has not been able to carry out. What shall I do now?"

He called for his retainers, and they consulted together. He told them: "You must think up a task that is beyond Emelyan's power. Whatever we have thought up so far he has done. And I haven't been able to take his wife away from him."

The counselors thought and thought. Then they came back to the Tsar and said, "You must send for Emelyan and tell him: 'Go I-don't-know-where and bring back I-don't-know-what.' He'll never be able to get out of that one! Wherever he goes, you can say it was the wrong place. And whatever he brings back, you can say it's the wrong thing. Then you can put him to death and take his wife."

The Tsar was delighted. "This time," he said, "you have really thought up something good."

He summoned Emelyan and told him: "Go I-don't-know-where and bring back I-don't-know-what. And if you don't bring it back, I'll cut off your head."

Emelyan went home to his wife and told her what the Tsar had said.

She became very thoughtful. "Well," she said, "this time they have taught the Tsar something that will cost them dear. But we must act wisely."

She sat and sat, and thought and thought, and at last

she said to her husband, "You must go far away to my grandmother, the old peasant woman, the mother of soldiers, and ask her for help. When she gives you something, go straight to the palace. I'll be there. I can't escape them now; they'll take me by force. But it won't be for long. If you do everything the old woman tells you to do, you will soon rescue me."

His wife got things ready for her husband's journey. She gave him a little bag, and she gave him her spindle. "Give this to the old woman," she said, "and she will know you are my husband."

She showed him the way to take, and he set off. When he had left the city behind him, he came upon some soldiers who were drilling. He stopped to watch them. The soldiers finished their drill and sat down to rest. Emelyan came up to them and asked: "Friends, can you tell me how to go I-don't-know-where and bring back I-don't-know-what?"

When the soldiers heard him say this, they were astounded. "Who sent you on such a quest?" they asked.

"The Tsar," he said.

"Ever since we became soldiers," they said, "we have been going I-don't-know-where, but we can't get there. And we have been looking for I-don't-know-what, and we can't find it. We can't help you."

Emelyan sat with the soldiers for a while and then continued on his way. He walked and walked, until he came to a forest. In the forest was a hut. In the hut sat a very old peasant woman, the mother of soldiers, spinning flax. She was weeping, and she did not put her fingers to her mouth to moisten them with spittle: she put them to her eyes to moisten them with tears.

When she saw Emelyan she cried out, "What have you come for?"

Emelyan gave her the spindle and told her that his wife had sent him. Immediately the old woman softened toward him and began asking questions. Then Emelyan started in telling her his whole life story: how he had married the maiden; how they had gone to the city to live; how he had been taken to the Tsar and made to work around the palace grounds; the kind of work he had done at the palace; how he had built a cathedral and a river with ships; and how, most recently, the Tsar had ordered him to go I-don't-know-where and bring back I-don't-know-what.

When she had heard what he had to say the old woman stopped crying. And she began muttering to herself, "Yes, the time has come. I can see that."

Then she said, "All right, my son. Sit down and eat."

When Emelyan had eaten, the old woman said to him, "Take this ball and roll it in front of you. Follow it wherever it goes. You will have a long way to go— all the way to the sea. When you come to the sea, you will find a big city. Go into the city and ask for a night's lodging in the farthest house. There you will look for the thing you need."

"But, Grandmother, how will I be able to know it?"

"When you see the thing that is obeyed better than

a father or mother is obeyed, that will be it. Seize it, and take it to the Tsar. When you bring it to him, he will say you have brought the wrong thing. Then you will say: 'If it's the wrong thing, it must be destroyed.' And you will strike the thing, and then carry it away to the river, smash it, and throw it into the water. Then you'll get your wife back, and my tears will be dried."

Emelyan said good-bye to the old woman and went off, rolling the ball. It rolled and rolled, and led him to the sea. On the edge of the sea there was a great city. At the edge of the city was a big house. Emelyan asked for a night's lodging, and they let him in. He lay down to sleep.

Early in the morning he awakened. He heard the

father rouse the son and ask him to go out and cut some wood. But the son did not obey his father. "It's still early," he said. "There's plenty of time."

Then he heard the mother, at the stove, say, "Go, my son. Your father's bones ache. Do you want him to go himself? It's time!"

But the son only smacked his lips and went back to sleep. No sooner had he dozed off than something began to rumble and rattle in the street. The son jumped out of bed, dressed, and ran out of the house. Emelyan, too, jumped up and ran after him. He wanted to see what was making the rumbling sound and what the son obeyed better than he did his father and mother.

He ran out, and he saw a man walking along the street, carrying on his belly a round object that he was beating with two sticks. That was the thing making the rumbling sound—the thing the son had obeyed! Emelyan ran up and began to examine the thing. He saw that it was round, like a little tub, with a skin stretched across either end. He asked what it was called.

"A drum," they told him.

"And it's empty?"

"It's empty," they said.

Emelyan was amazed. He asked if he could have the drum, but they refused him. So he stopped asking and began to follow the drummer. He walked after him the whole day, and when the drummer lay down to sleep, he seized the drum and ran off with it.

He ran and ran till he reached home. He had thought he would find his wife there, but she was gone. The day after Emelyan left they had taken her to the Tsar.

He went to the palace and told them to announce him. "Tell him," he said, "that he has come who has been I-don't-know-where, and that he has brought back I-don't-know-what."

They announced him to the Tsar, but the Tsar sent back word that he should return the next day. Emelyan asked to be announced again. "I have come today," he said, "and I have brought what he ordered me to bring. If the Tsar doesn't come out to me, I will go in to him."

The Tsar came out. "Where have you been?" he asked.

Emelyan told him.

"That was the wrong place," the Tsar said. "And what have you brought back?"

Emelyan tried to show him, but the Tsar didn't look. "That's the wrong thing," he said.

"If it's the wrong thing, it must be destroyed," said Emelyan. "And the devil take it!"

He walked out of the palace, beating the drum as he went. As soon as he started drumming, all of the Tsar's troops assembled around him. They saluted him and waited for his command.

From a window the Tsar shouted to his troops not to follow Emelyan. But they paid no heed to the Tsar: all of them followed Emelyan.

When the Tsar saw this he gave orders that Emelyan's wife should be returned to him. And he asked Emelyan to give him the drum.

"I can't," said Emelyan. "I have orders to destroy it and throw it into the river."

He marched to the river with the drum, and all of the soldiers followed him. At the river's edge he knocked a hole in the drum, broke it into little pieces, and threw them into the water. Whereupon the soldiers ran away in all directions.

Then Emelyan took his wife and went home with her.

From that day on the Tsar ceased to bother him. And he lived happily ever after, enduring the bad and enjoying the good.

*A
Grain
the Size of
a Hen's
Egg*

Some children once found, in a ravine, a thing the size of a hen's egg that had a groove in the middle like a kernel of grain. A passer-by noticed what the children had found. He gave them five kopecks for it, took it into the city, and sold it to the Tsar because it was something rare.

The Tsar called for his wise men and told them to find out what the thing was: an egg, or a kernel of grain. The wise men thought and thought about it, but couldn't tell which it was. Meantime, a hen flew up to the window ledge where the thing was lying, and began to peck at it. She pecked a hole in it, and then everybody saw that it was a kernel. The wise men went to the Tsar and told him, "It is a grain of rye."

The Tsar was amazed. He commanded the wise men to find out where and when such a grain had been grown. The wise men thought long and hard about it, and they searched through their books. But they couldn't find out anything.

They went back to the Tsar and said, "We can't answer the question. There is nothing about it in our books. We'll have to ask the peasants whether any of them has ever heard from one of the old men where and when such seeds were sown."

So the Tsar commanded some of his men to find a very old peasant and bring him to the city. They found one and brought him before the Tsar. He was so old that his face had a greenish color, he had no teeth, and he hobbled along with difficulty on two crutches.

The Tsar showed him the kernel. But the old man could hardly see any more; so he half peered at it, and half felt it with his hands. Then the Tsar asked him, "Can you tell us, old man, where this grain came from? Did you ever sow such seeds in your own field? Or have you ever bought such seeds in your lifetime?"

The old man was almost deaf. It was very, very hard for him to hear or understand. "No," he said, "in my field I never sowed or reaped such grain. And never did I buy any seed like that. The kind I bought were always small. You'd better ask my father. Maybe he knows where such grain grows."

The Tsar sent for the old man's father, and he was brought before him. The old man walked with one crutch. The Tsar showed him the kernel. The old man's eyes were still sharp, and he could see things very well.

The Tsar asked him, "Can you tell us, old man, where this kernel comes from? Did you ever sow such seeds in your own field? Or have you ever bought such seeds in your lifetime?"

The old man was partly deaf, but he still heard better than his son. "No," he said, "in my field I never sowed or reaped such grain. And I never bought any, because in my day there was no such thing as money. We all had enough to eat from the grain we raised ourselves. Or if somebody was in need of it, we would share. I don't know where that kernel was grown. It is true that the kernels of our grain were bigger than what they grow today, and we got more grain and less straw when we threshed. But still, I never saw one like that. I've heard my father say, though, that in his day the grain grew better than ours. The kernels were bigger, and they got more of them when they threshed. So you'd better ask him."

The Tsar sent for the old man's father. His men found this ancient man, and brought him to the Tsar. He walked up without any crutches. His step was springy, his eyes were bright, his hearing was very good and he spoke very clearly.

The Tsar showed him the kernel. The grandfather looked at it for a while, turning it over in his hands. Then he said, "It's been a long time since I've seen any of this old-fashioned grain."

He took a bite of the kernel and chewed on it for a while. "That's it, all right," he said.

"Tell me, Grandpa," asked the Tsar. "Where and when did people grow grain like this? In your field, did you ever sow such seeds? Or have you ever bought any such in your lifetime?"

And the old man answered, "In my day we grew grain like this everywhere. I fed myself with it, and I fed others with it. I sowed grain like this, and reaped it, and threshed it."

"Then tell me, Grandpa, did you ever buy any such

seed anywhere, or did you grow it in your own field?"

The old man laughed. "In my time," he said, "nobody could even have thought of such a sin as selling or buying grain. As for money, we had never heard of it. Everybody had all the food he needed."

"Where did you sow such grain, Grandpa?" asked the Tsar. "Where was your field?"

And the grandfather answered, "My field was God's earth. Wherever I plowed, that was my field. The land was for everybody. Nobody ever claimed it as his own. The only thing a man called his own was the work he did."

"Then tell me two things more," said the Tsar. "First, why is it that people used to grow such kernels of grain, but don't grow them now? Second, why is it that your grandson came in on two crutches, and your son on one crutch, but you came in walking very easily. Your eyes are bright, your teeth are good, and your voice is clear and hearty. Just how is it, Grandpa, that these things have come to pass?"

And the old man said, "These things have come to pass because men ceased to live by their own work and began wanting to live off the work of others. In the old days we lived by God's law; we used what was ours, and didn't covet what was our neighbor's."

A Story for
Children

A little girl and a little boy were traveling in a carriage from one village to another. The girl was five years old, and the boy was six. They were cousins, their mothers being sisters. They were going home with a nursemaid, while their mothers stayed behind with the people they had been visiting.

As they were passing through one village, a wheel on the carriage broke, and the coachman said they would have to stop while he repaired it. "It happened at a good time," the nursemaid said, "because we have been travelling for quite some time, now, and the children are hungry. Since we're getting out here, I can give them some bread and milk."

It was a cold, rainy day in autumn. The nursemaid and the children went into the nearest peasant hut. Inside the hut it was dirty and smoky, because there was no chimney for the stove. When this kind of hut is heated in the cold weather, they just open the door and let the smoke out that way until the fire in the stove is going well. This particular hut was old and dirty, with chinks in the floor. In one corner there was a small image of a saint, with a bench and table under it. Across from it was the big stove.

But what the children noticed first of all was two youngsters about their own age: a barefoot girl wearing only a dirty blouse, and a nearly-naked boy with a big belly. A third child—a baby girl about one year old—

was lying on a coffer-bench, drenched in tears. Her mother had been trying to quiet her. But when the nursemaid came in with the two children she left off and busied herself with making a place for them at the table and bench in the front corner.

The nursemaid had brought with her from the carriage a bag with a shiny lock on it. The peasant children stared at the lock in wonder, each one pointing it out to the other. The nursemaid brought out a bottle of warm milk, a loaf of bread, and a clean napkin, and laid them on the table. "Come to the table, children," she said, "you must be hungry."

But the children didn't move. Sonya, the girl, was staring at the peasant children, looking from one to the other. She had never seen such dirty blouses or such naked children, and was astounded at them. Petya, the boy, was looking first at Sonya, then at the peasant children, not knowing whether he should laugh or show his astonishment. Sonya stared especially hard at the baby girl on the coffer-bench, who was crying loudly.

"Why is she crying?" she asked.

"She's hungry," her mother said.

"Then give her something to eat."

"I would, but there isn't anything."

"Come on, children," the nursemaid said, busily laying out the bread on the table. "Come on, come on!" she repeated angrily.

They obeyed her and went to the table. She poured
milk into glasses and offered it to them, along with a
piece of bread. But Sonya, refusing to eat, pushed her
glass away. Petya, who had been watching her, did the
same thing.

"Is it true?" Sonya asked, indicating the mother.

"Is what true?" the nursemaid asked.

"That she doesn't have any milk," Sonya said.

"Who knows? It's none of our business. But you must eat."

"I won't," Sonya said.

"I won't either," Petya said.

"Give it to her," said Sonya, still looking at the baby girl.

"Enough of your nonsense," the nursemaid said. "Eat, or it'll get cold."

"I won't eat! I won't!" Sonya cried out suddenly. "I won't even eat when we get home, unless you give her something."

"You eat first, and I'll give her what's left."

"I won't—not until you give her something."

"I won't either! I won't either!" Petya repeated. "Not for anything. I won't!"

The nursemaid said, "That's a lot of nonsense you've got into your heads, and you're talking nonsense now. Do you think everybody can be equal? God is generous to some people. He was generous to you and your father."

"Why wasn't he generous to them?" Sonya asked.

"It's not for us to judge. Such was the will of God," the nursemaid said, and then poured some milk into a cup and handed it to the peasant woman so she could give it to the baby. The baby began to drink the milk, and quieted down. But Sonya still refused to eat or to drink.

"The will of God," she repeated. "But why did He

Leo Tolstoy's

will a thing like that? Bad God! Horrible God! Just for
that, I'm not going to pray to Him any more!"

The nursemaid shook her head. "You're saying
naughty things. I'll have to tell your father."

"Go ahead and tell him," Sonya said. "I've made up
my mind. I've made up my mind about everything. It's
wrong. It's all wrong."

"What's wrong?" asked the nursemaid.

"That some people have a lot while other people don't
have anything."

"Maybe it's on purpose," Petya said.

"No. Bad, bad! I won't drink anything, and I won't
eat anything. Bad God! I don't love Him."

Suddenly, from behind the stove, they heard a cough,
and then a hoarse voice said, "Ah, children, children!
You are good children, but what you're saying isn't
right."

There was more coughing. The children peered at
the stove and saw, leaning down from the stove-bench
above, a wrinkled old man with gray hair. He shook his
head and said, "God is not bad, little ones—He is good.
He loves everybody. If some people have fancy bread
to eat and others don't have any, it's not His fault. It's
something that people did. And they did it because they
forgot Him." There was more coughing, then, "They've
forgotten Him, and that's why they've done it. They've
forgotten that some people live well, with more than
they need, while other people just drag along more

dead than alive. But if they all lived like good Christians, then everybody would have enough of everything."

"But," asked Sonya, "what should we do so that everybody has enough of everything?"

"What should you do?" the old man mumbled. "Do what God commands. And God commands us to share, and share alike."

"What? What?" Petya asked.

"God commands us to share, and share alike."

"Share and share alike," Petya repeated. "When I grow up, that's what I'll do."

"I will, too," Sonya added.

"I said it first," Petya told her. "I'll fix things so nobody is poor."

"Enough of your foolishness," the nursemaid said. "Drink what's left of your milk."

"We won't! We won't," both of the children said in one voice. "And when we grow up, we'll do just what we said."

"Good for you, little ones!" said the old man. And he smiled, showing only two lower teeth. "I won't live long enough to see what you do. But you've got the right idea. God help you!"

"They can do whatever they want with us," Sonya said, "but we'll do what we said."

"We'll do what we said," Petya repeated.

"Now you're talking!" said the old man, laughing and then starting to cough. "Probably I'll be watching you with pleasure from up there," he managed to say, when his coughing had stopped. "Keep an eye out, and don't forget."

"We won't," the children said.

"Just be true to your word, that's all."

The coachman came in to report that the wheel was fixed, and the children left.

What will happen in the future? We'll see.

The Tale of
Ivan the Fool
and His Two Brothers,
Semyon the Soldier and
Taras the Big-Belly,
and of His Sister,
Malanya the Deaf-Mute,
and of the Old Devil
and the Three Imps

*I*n a certain kingdom in a certain land there once lived a rich peasant. And the rich peasant had three sons—Semyon the Soldier, Taras the Big-Belly, and Ivan the Fool—and one daughter, Malanya the Deaf-Mute. Semyon the Soldier went to war to serve the Tsar, Taras the Big-Belly went to a merchant's in the city to become a trader, and Ivan the Fool stayed home with his sister to work in the fields.

Semyon the Soldier won high rank and an estate, and married a nobleman's daughter. His pay was big and his estate was big, but he still couldn't make ends meet. Whatever he took in, his high-born wife squandered it all, and they never had any money.

When Semyon went to his estate to collect the income, his steward said to him, "We don't have anything to earn money with. We don't have any horses, or milk cows, or other livestock, or tools, or a plow or harrow. We must get these first—then there'll be an income."

So Semyon the Soldier went to his father. "You are rich, Father," he said, "but you have never given me anything. Give me a third of what you have, and I'll add it to my estate."

But the old man said, "You never made any contribution when you were here at home. Why should I give you a third? It wouldn't be fair to Ivan and the girl."

Semyon said, "But after all, he's a fool and she's deaf and dumb. What good is it to them?"

Then the old man said, "It's up to Ivan."

And Ivan said, "Well, why not? Let him take it."

So Semyon the Soldier took the portion of his father's property and added it to his own estate, and then went off to serve the Tsar again.

Taras the Big-Belly also acquired a lot of money, and married a merchant's daughter. But his income still wasn't enough; so he came to his father and said, "Give me my share."

But the old man was not willing to give Taras his portion, either. "You never contributed anything when you were here at home. Everything in this house was brought in by Ivan. Besides, it wouldn't be fair to him and the girl."

But Taras said, "What good is it to him? He's a fool. He'll never get married, because nobody will have him. And a girl who's a deaf-mute doesn't need anything, either. Come on, Ivan," he said. "Give me half of the grain, and as for the livestock, all I want to take is the big gray stallion. You can't use him for plowing, anyway."

Ivan laughed. "Well, why not?" he said. "I'll go and put a halter on him."

So they gave Taras his portion, too. He hauled the grain into town, and led away the gray stallion. Ivan was left with one old gray mare to go on with his farming as before—and to feed his father and mother and Malanya.

II

Now the Old Devil was most annoyed that the three brothers had not quarreled over the divvying-up, but had parted affectionately. So he summoned the three imps. "Now listen to me," he said. "There are three brothers: Semyon the Soldier, Taras the Big-Belly, and Ivan the Fool. They all should have quarreled, but instead they're living in peace and on good terms. The Fool upset all of my plans. I want the three of you to go out and take on the three of them. Get them so worked up they'll tear each other's eyes out. Can you do that?"

"We can do it," the three imps said.

"How will you go about it?"

"Like this," they said. "First we'll make them so poor they won't have a crust of bread to nibble on. Then we'll throw them together in a heap, and they'll start fighting."

"All right," the Old Devil said. "I see you know your business. Get going. And don't come back until all three of them are at loggerheads. Otherwise I'll skin all three of you alive."

The imps went off to a swamp to discuss how they should go at this business. They argued and argued, each one trying to get the easiest job. Finally they decided to draw straws to determine who would take on whom. And if one finished his job first, he was supposed to help the others. They drew straws, and then set a time when they would again meet in the swamp to find out who had finished his job, and whom he should help.

When the time came, the imps assembled in the swamp as agreed. Each one began to explain how things were going with him. The first imp started telling about Semyon the Soldier.

"My job is coming along fine," he said. "Tomorrow Semyon will be going home to his father."

His brothers began to question him. "How did you manage it?" they asked.

"Well," he said, "the first thing I did was to instill so much bravery into Semyon that he promised his Tsar he would conquer the whole world. So the Tsar made him a commanding general and sent him to do battle with the king of India. The battle lines were drawn up. But during the night I dampened all the gunpowder that Semyon's army had. Then I went to the king of India, and for him I made more straw soldiers than can possibly be imagined. When Semyon's soldiers saw the straw soldiers coming at them from every side, they took fright. Semyon gave orders to fire, but the artillery and the rifles wouldn't discharge. Semyon's soldiers panicked and fled like sheep, and the king of India defeated them.

"Now Semyon the Soldier is in disgrace; the people have taken away his estate, and they intend to execute him tomorrow. I have only one day's work left—to get him out of prison so he can run home. My job will be finished then. Now tell me, which one of you two needs help?"

The second imp—the one assigned to Taras—began telling about his work. "I don't need any help," he said. "My job has come along very well, too. Taras won't hold out for more than another week. The first thing I did was to make his belly still bigger and fill him with envious greed. He developed so much envy for the things other people had, that he wanted to buy whatever he saw. He spent all his money buying immense quantities of things, and he's still buying—except that now it's with borrowed money. By this time he has a load of debts. A week from now his payments will be due, but I'll turn all his merchandise into manure. He won't be able to pay, and he'll go home to his father."

Then they began to question the third imp about Ivan. "How is your work coming along?" they asked.

"To tell the truth," he said, "it isn't going very well. The first thing I did was to spit in his jug of kvass so he'd have a stomach-ache. Then I went to the field he was plowing, and pounded the earth until it was as hard as stone, so he wouldn't be able to plow it. I was sure he couldn't. But, fool that he is, he came with his wooden plow and began making a furrow. He groaned with the pain in his stomach, but he kept right on plowing. I broke that one plow, but the idiot went home, rigged up another one, and started plowing again. I crawled under the ground and grabbed onto the plowshare, but there was no holding it back: the Fool leaned hard on the plow, and the plowshare was sharp—it cut my hands all over. By now he's plowed almost the whole field; there's only one little strip left. Come and help me, fellows," he said, "because if we don't get the better of him, all our labor will be lost. If that fool keeps on farming, none of them will be really up against it, because he'll feed both of his brothers."

III

Ivan had plowed almost all of the fallow land. Only one little strip was left, and he went out to finish it. His stomach ached, but the plowing had to be done.

Ivan let the harness ropes go slack, flipped the plow over, and started plowing. He had just made one furrow and headed back when the plow began to drag as if it was caught on a root. Actually, it was the imp, who had twined his legs around the plowshare and was holding it back. That's funny, Ivan thought. There wasn't any root there before, but now there is.

He reached down into the furrow and felt something soft. He grabbed it, and pulled it out. It was black, like a root; but on that root something was wriggling. Lo and behold! a live imp!

"Just look at you!" said Ivan. "How disgusting!"

He raised his hand, and was about to smash the imp on the plow handle, but the imp squealed: "Don't hit me! I'll do whatever you want!"

"What will you do for me?"

"Anything you want—just tell me."

Ivan scratched himself. "My belly aches," he said. "Can you fix it?"

"Yes," said the imp.

"Well then, fix it."

The imp bent over and scratched around in the furrow with his claws. He scratched around some more, then he pulled out a little three-pronged root and handed it to Ivan. "Here," he said. "Whenever anybody eats one of these little roots, all his pains go away."

Ivan took it, tore it apart, and swallowed one of the rootlets. His stomach-ache vanished immediately.

The imp began to plead again. "Let me go," he said. "If you do, I'll jump into the earth and never walk on top of it again."

"Well, why not?" said Ivan. "I don't care what you do, God knows."

No sooner had Ivan mentioned God than the imp sank down into the earth like a stone into water, and nothing remained but a hole. Ivan stuck the other two roots in his cap and set about finishing his plowing. When he had plowed the rest of the strip, he flipped the plow over and went home.

He unharnessed the mare, and went into the hut. There sat his older brother, Semyon the Soldier, and his wife—eating supper. Semyon's estate had been taken away from him; he had barely managed to escape from prison; and he had come running home to live with his father.

When Semyon saw Ivan he said, "I've come to live with you. Feed me and my wife until a new position opens up for me."

"Well, why not?" said Ivan. "You're welcome to live here."

He was about to sit down on the bench, but the high-born lady objected to his smell. "I simply cannot eat," she said, "at the same table with a stinking peasant."

And Semyon the Soldier said, "My lady says you don't smell good. You'd better go eat in the hallway."

"Well, why not?" said Ivan. "Anyway, it's time for the night watch. I have to put the mare out to pasture."

He took some bread, picked up his coat, and went out for the night watch in the pasture.

IV

Semyon the Soldier's imp, having finished his job that night, came looking for Ivan's imp to help him get the better of the Fool. He came to the plowed field and looked and looked for his brother, but found only a hole in the ground. Well, he thought, it looks as though my brother ran into trouble, so I'll have to take his place. And the plowing is all done, so I'll have to get the better of the Fool while he's mowing the hay.

The imp went to the meadow and flooded the entire crop of hay so that it was all covered with mud. At daybreak, Ivan returned from his night watch, sharpened a scythe, and went to the meadow to mow. He had only swung the scythe a couple of times when it became dull and in need of sharpening again. Ivan struggled and struggled, but finally he said, "Enough of this. I'll go home and get the whetstone and bring it out here with me. And I'll bring along a loaf of bread. Even if it takes me a week of hard work, I'm not leaving until this hay is mowed."

The imp heard him, and thought, "This fool is a tough nut to crack. I'll have to try some other tricks."

Ivan came back, whetted the scythe, and began to mow. The imp crawled into the uncut hay and began grabbing the scythe by the heel, driving the tip of the blade into the ground. It was hard going for Ivan, but he mowed all of the hay except one small patch in a bog. The imp crawled into the bog, thinking to himself, "Even if I get my paws cut off, I won't let him finish mowing."

Ivan went into the swamp. He could see that the grass there wasn't thick; and yet he couldn't cut through it. He grew angry and started swinging with all his might. The imp began to give up—he just couldn't get out of the way fast enough on the backswing. Seeing it was no use, he hid himself in a bush. Ivan swung the scythe and grazed the bush, cutting off half the imp's tail.

When he had finished mowing the hay, Ivan told his sister to rake it while he went to mow the rye.

He went to the rye field with his sickle; but the bob-tailed imp had got there first and tangled up the rye so badly that the sickle wouldn't cut. Ivan went back, brought a reaping-hook, and started cutting down the rye with that. He reaped all of it.

"Now," he said, "it's time to go to work on the oats."

The bobtailed imp heard him and thought, "I didn't get the better of him on the rye, but I will on the oats. Just wait till morning!"

The next morning the imp hurried out to the oat field, but the oats were already cut. Ivan had harvested them at night. The imp was furious. He said to himself, "That Fool has cut me up and worn me out. Not even in war did I ever see such calamities. He never sleeps, damn him! You just can't keep up with him. But now I'll get into the shocks and rot all of them for him."

So the imp went up to a shock of rye, crawled in among the sheaves, and began rotting them. He warmed them up, but he warmed himself at the same time, and dozed off.

Meantime, Ivan harnessed the mare and went with his sister to bring in the rye. He came to that particular shock where the imp was sleeping and began pitching the sheaves onto the cart. He pitched up two of them, stuck his fork in again—and jabbed the imp right in the rear end! He raised up the fork, and lo and behold! on the prongs was a live imp—and a bobtailed one at that—wriggling, making horrible faces, and trying to get off the hook!

"Just look at you!" Ivan said. "How disgusting! Are you back again?"

"I'm not the same one," the imp said. "That was my

brother. And I used to be with your own brother Semyon."

"Well," said Ivan, "whoever you are, you're going to get the same thing he got." And he was about to smash him on the edge of the hayrack when the imp began to plead with him.

"Let me go!" he said. "I won't bother you any more, and I'll do whatever you want me to."

"And what can you do?"

"Well," he said, "for one thing I can make soldiers out of almost anything."

"But what are they good for?"

"Why, for whatever you want. They can do anything."

"Can they play tunes?"

"Oh, yes!"

"Well then, make some."

Then the imp said, "Take that sheaf of rye there and shake it over the ground, bottom down, and then say: *By my bondman's decree, let his sheaf cease to be. And let there be as many soldiers as there are straws in thee.*"

Ivan took the sheaf and shook it over the ground, uttering the words the imp had told him to say. The sheaf burst apart and turned into soldiers, with a drummer and buglers marching in front.

Ivan laughed. "Just look at that!" he said. "How clever! Just dandy! The girls will enjoy it."

"Well, then," the imp said, "let me go now."

"No," said Ivan, "I'll make them out of straw. That way, the grain won't be wasted. Show me how to turn them back into a sheaf. Then I'll thresh it."

So the imp told him: "Just say: *Let there be as many straws as there are soldiers now. By my bondman's decree, let this sheaf once more be.*"

Ivan said the words, and the sheaf reappeared.

"Now let me go," the imp said.

"Well, why not?"

Ivan hooked him onto the edge of the hayrack, took hold of him with one hand, and pulled him off the pitchfork. "God be with you," he said.

As soon as he mentioned God, the imp sank into the ground like a stone into water, and nothing remained but a hole.

Ivan went home, and there he found his other brother, Taras, sitting at supper with his wife. Taras the Big-Belly hadn't managed to pay his debts, and had run home to his father. When he saw Ivan he said, "What do you say, Ivan? Can you feed me and my wife until I get back on my feet?"

"Well, why not?" said Ivan. "You're welcome to live here."

He took off his coat and sat down at the table. But the merchant's daughter said: "I can't eat at the same table with the Fool. He reeks," said she, "of sweat."

And Taras the Big-Belly said, "Ivan, you smell bad. You'd better go eat in the hallway."

"Well, why not?" said Ivan. He took some bread and

headed out the door. "Besides," he said, "it's time to pasture the mare for the night."

V

That night Taras's imp came to help his brothers get the better of Ivan the Fool. He came to the plowed field and looked and looked for them, but there wasn't anyone there—just a hole in the ground. He went to the hayfield, and in the bog he found a tail, and near a shock of rye he found another hole. "Well," he told himself, "it's plain to see that they ran into trouble. I'll have to take their place and get to work on the Fool."

The imp went looking for Ivan. But Ivan had already finished up the work in the harvest fields and was in the grove cutting down trees. (Ivan's two brothers had begun to feel cramped living together, so they had told the Fool to keep the hut for himself and go out and fell some trees and build new houses for them.)

The imp hurried to the grove, crawled up into the branches of a tree, and began to hinder Ivan at his work. Ivan had undercut a tree so it would fall clear, and then chopped through it. But it fell the wrong way and got caught in some branches. He cut off a pole, pried the tree loose, and finally managed to bring it down. He started felling another tree, and the same thing happened: he struggled and struggled, and barely managed to free it. He went to work on a third tree, and again the same thing happened.

Ivan had intended to cut down about fifty young

trees; but night settled over the farm before he had even brought down a dozen. And he was exhausted. Steam rose from him and spread through the woods like a fog, but still he would not quit. He undercut one more tree, but then his back began to ache so painfully that he couldn't stand it. He drove his axe into the tree and sat down to rest.

When the imp saw that Ivan had stopped working, he was delighted. Well, he thought, he's worn out—he'll give up now, and I can get a rest, too.

He sat down astride a branch, rejoicing. But Ivan got up, pulled out his axe, and hauled off and hit the tree from the other side with such force that it immediately began to sway, and then crashed down. The imp was caught off guard; he couldn't get his leg free in time. The branch broke off, and trapped the imp by his paw.

Ivan had begun stripping the tree when, lo and behold! a live imp!

Ivan was amazed. "Just look at you!" he said. "How disgusting! Are you back again?"

"I'm not the same one," he said. "I was with your brother Taras."

"Well, whoever you are, you're going to get the same thing he got!"

Ivan brandished his axe, and was about to beat the imp with the butt end.

"Don't hit me!" he pleaded. "I'll do whatever you want."

"And what can you do?"

"Well," he said, "for one thing I can create money for you—as much as you want."

"Well, then," said Ivan, "make some."

So the imp showed him how. "Take a leaf from this oak tree," he said, "and rub it in your hands; gold will fall to the ground."

Ivan took some leaves and rubbed them; a shower of gold fell on the ground. "This is dandy," he said, "for playing games with children."

"Then let me go," the imp said.

"Well, why not?" He took his pole and pried the imp free, saying, "I don't care what you do, God knows."

No sooner had he mentioned God than the imp sank into the ground like a stone into water, and nothing remained but a hole.

VI

The brothers had built their houses and were living separately. Meanwhile, having finished with the harvest work and brewed some beer, Ivan invited his brothers to celebrate with him. But they wouldn't come. "We are not accustomed," they said, "to joining in the celebrations of peasants."

So Ivan invited some peasants and their wives. He himself drank heartily, grew tipsy, and went out into the street where people were singing and dancing. He went up to them and told the women to sing a song in his praise. "Then," he said, "I'll give you something you've never seen before in your life." The women laughed, and sang a song praising him. When they had finished they said, "Well, let's have it!"

"I'll bring it," he said, "right now." And he grabbed a seed bag and ran off to the woods.

"He really is a fool!" the women said, laughing. And they forgot about him. But behold! Ivan was running back, carrying the seed bag full of something.

"Should I give it out?"

"Yes, give it out!"

Ivan took a handful of gold and threw it at the women. Lord, how they rushed to pick it up! And up came the men, scrambling and fighting over it. One old woman was almost crushed to death.

Ivan laughed. "Oh, you fools!" he said. "Why crush the old granny? Take it easy—I'll give you more." And he began to scatter more of it. They scrambled for the gold and Ivan emptied the whole bag.

Then he said, "That's all. I'll give you more some other time. Now let's have some songs and dancing."

The women struck up a song.

"Your songs are no good," he said.

"What songs are better?" they asked.

"I'll show you," he said. "Right now."

He went to the barn and got a sheaf of grain. He beat out the grain, stood the sheaf on its bottom end, and tapped it. "Now," he said, "*My serf would as lief thou wert no more a sheaf, but every straw a soldier.*"

The sheaf burst apart, and turned into soldiers playing drums and bugles. Ivan ordered the soldiers to play a march, and then he led them out into the street. The people were amazed. The soldiers played some more tunes, and then Ivan led them back to the barn, saying nobody should follow them. There he turned the soldiers back into a sheaf, and threw it back on the pile. Then he went home and lay down to sleep in the stable.

VII

The next morning the eldest brother, Semyon the Soldier, heard about these things and went to see Ivan. "Tell me," he said, "where did you get those soldiers? And where did you take them?"

"Why do you want to know?" Ivan asked.

"What do you mean, *why?* With soldiers, a man can do anything. He can win a kingdom for himself."

Ivan was astonished. "Is that so? Why didn't you tell me a long time ago? I'll make you as many soldiers as you want. Thank goodness we threshed a lot—I mean the girl and me."

Ivan took his brother to the barn and said, "Look, I'll make them for you, but then you'll have to take them away from here. Because if we had to feed them they'd gobble up the whole village in one day."

Semyon the Soldier promised to lead the troops away, and Ivan began to make them. He tapped one sheaf on the floor—and there was a company. He tapped another sheaf—and there was another company. He made so many that they covered an entire field.

"Well, that should be about enough, shouldn't it?"

Semyon was overjoyed. He said, "Yes, that's enough. Thank you, Ivan."

"All right. If you need any more, just come back here and I'll make more. I have a lot of straw right now."

Semyon the Soldier immediately gave orders to his troops, mustered them in proper fashion, and went off to make war.

No sooner had Semyon the Soldier left than Taras the Big-Belly showed up. He, too, had heard about what happened the day before, and he asked his brother: "Tell me, where did you get those gold coins? If I had that much cash on hand, I'd use it to bring in money from all over the world!"

Ivan was astonished. "Is that so? You should have told me a long time ago. I'll rub you as much money as you want."

His brother was delighted. "Give me about three sacks of it."

"Well, why not?" said Ivan. "Let's go to the woods. But you'd better harness up the horse first. You won't be able to carry it by yourself."

They went into the woods, and Ivan began to rub leaves from the oak tree. Soon there was a big pile of gold.

"That should be about enough, shouldn't it?"

Taras was overjoyed. "It will do for the time being," he said. "Thank you, Ivan."

"All right," said Ivan. "If you need any more, just

come back here and I'll rub some more—there are plenty of leaves left."

Taras the Big-Belly gathered up the money—a whole cartload—and went off to trade.

So the two brothers went away: Semyon to wage war, and Taras to trade. Semyon the Soldier won a kingdom for himself, and Taras the Big-Belly made a heap of money buying and selling.

The two brothers got together and revealed their secrets to each other: where Semyon had got his soldiers, and where Taras had got his money.

And Semyon the Soldier said to his brother, "I have conquered a kingdom for myself, and I live well, but I don't have enough money to feed my soldiers."

Taras the Big-Belly said, "And I have made a great heap of money. But there's just one trouble: I don't have anybody to guard it."

Then Semyon the Soldier said, "Let's go see brother Ivan. I'll order him to make more soldiers, and then I'll give them to you to guard your money. And you can order him to rub me more money so I'll have the wherewithal to feed my soldiers."

And so they went to see Ivan. When they got there, Semyon said: "Brother mine, I still don't have enough soldiers. Make me some more—from as many sheaves as there are in a couple of shocks, say."

Ivan shook his head. "You're wasting your breath," he said. "I won't make any more soldiers for you."

"But why? After all, you promised."

"I know. But I won't make any more,."

"But why won't you, you fool?"

"Because your soldiers killed a man dead. The other day when I was going near the road I saw a woman coming down the road hauling a coffin, and she was wailing. 'Who died?' I asked her. And she said, 'Semyon's soldiers killed my husband in the war.' I thought the soldiers would play tunes, but they've killed a man dead. So I won't give you any more."

And he stood firm, and made no more soldiers.

Then Taras the Big-Belly began pleading with Ivan the Fool to make him more gold coins.

Ivan shook his head. "You're wasting your breath," he said. "I won't make any more."

"But why won't you, you fool?"

"Because your gold pieces took away Mikhailovna's cow."

"What do you mean, *took it away?*"

"They just took it away, that's all. Mikhailovna had a cow, and her children used to drink the milk. The other day they came to me asking for milk. I asked them, 'Where is your cow?' And they said, 'Taras the Big-Belly's steward came and gave Mamma three pieces of gold, and she gave him the cow, so now we don't have any milk to drink.' I thought you only wanted to play games with the gold pieces, but you took away the children's cow. So I won't give you any more."

And the Fool stood firm, and wouldn't give any more. So the two brothers went away, and began to consider how they might help each other in their troubles. And Semyon said, "I'll tell you what we'll do. You give me money to feed my soldiers, and I'll give you half of my kingdom and soldiers to guard your money."

Taras agreed. The brothers divided their possessions, and both became tsars, and both were rich.

VIII

Meantime, Ivan lived at home, feeding his father and mother and working in the fields with the mute girl.

Now it happened that Ivan's old watchdog got sick, became mangy, and was about to die. Ivan felt sorry for her. He got some bread from his sister, Malanya, put it in his cap, took it out to the dog, and threw it to her. But the cap was torn, and along with the bread, a root fell out. The aged dog gobbled it up together with the bread. No sooner had it swallowed the root, than it jumped up and started to play—wagging its tail and barking. It had recovered completely!

Ivan's father and mother saw this, and they were amazed. "How did you cure the dog?" they asked.

And Ivan said, "I had two little roots that cure any pain, and it gobbled up one of them."

At that same time it happened that the Tsar's daughter fell ill. The Tsar caused it to be announced in all cities and hamlets that whosoever cured her would receive an award and, if he were a bachelor, would be given her hand in marriage. The announcement was made in Ivan's village, too.

His father called Ivan in and said to him, "Did you hear what the Tsar has announced? You were saying that you had one of those little roots left. Go and cure the Tsar's daughter, and you'll be happy the rest of your life."

"Well, why not?" he said.

And Ivan got ready to go. His father and mother helped him dress up, and he had just stepped out of the door when he saw a beggar woman with a crippled arm. "They tell me," she said, "that you can cure people. Heal my arm—otherwise I can't even put on my boots myself."

And Ivan said, "Well, why not?"

He took the little root, gave it to the beggar woman, and told her to swallow it. She swallowed it, was cured, and began waving her arm.

Ivan's father and mother came out to accompany him on his trip to see the Tsar. When they heard he had given his last root away and had nothing left to cure the Tsar's daughter with, they began to upbraid him. "You took pity on the beggar woman," they said, "but for the Tsar's daughter you have no pity!"

Ivan began to feel sorry for the Tsar's daughter, too. He harnessed up the horse, threw some straw into the cart, and climbed in, ready to set off.

"Where are you going, Fool?"

"To heal the Tsar's daughter."

"When you have nothing to heal her with?"

"Well, why not?" he said, and gave the horse a flick of the reins.

He arrived at the Tsar's palace, and no sooner had he set foot on the steps than the Tsar's daughter recovered.

The Tsar was overjoyed. He summoned Ivan, had him dressed in fine clothing, and rewarded him. "Be my son-in-law," he said.

"Well, why not?" said Ivan.

So he married the Tsar's daughter. Not long afterwards the Tsar died, and Ivan became Tsar. So now all three brothers were tsars.

IX

The three brothers lived and reigned.

The eldest brother, Semyon the Soldier, lived very well. He drafted real soldiers to add to his straw soldiers. He decreed that throughout his realm, one household out of every ten must supply a soldier; and that every soldier must be tall, physically fit, and clear-eyed. He recruited many such soldiers, and trained them all. Whenever anybody opposed his designs, he immediately dispatched these soldiers, and did whatever he wanted. So everybody began to fear him.

His life was most pleasant. Whatever he thought of, or whatever he laid eyes on, was his. He would send out his soldiers, and they would seize and bring back whatever he wanted.

Taras the Big-Belly also lived very well. He had not

wasted the money he had got from Ivan, but had made lots more with it. In his kingdom he had set up a fine system. He kept his own money in coffers, and collected a poll tax, and a vodka tax, and a beer tax, and a wedding tax, and a funeral tax, and a tax for traveling on foot, and a tax for traveling on horseback, and a tax on bast shoes, and a tax on leg wrappings, and a tax on dress trimmings. And whatever he took a mind to, was his. For money, people would procure anything for him and do anything for him, because everybody needs money.

Ivan the Fool didn't live badly either. As soon as he had buried his father-in-law he took off all his royal attire, gave it to his wife to put away in a trunk, and got back into his peasant's shirt, peasant-style pants, and bast shoes, and got ready to work. "I'm bored," he said. "I'm getting a paunch, don't have any appetite, and I can't sleep."

He sent for his mother and father and sister, the mute girl, and started working again.

"But you're the Tsar!" people told him.

"Well, what's the difference?" he said. "Tsars have to eat, too."

A cabinet minister came to him and said, "We don't have any money to pay salaries to our officials."

"Well, what's the difference?" he said. "Don't pay them."

"But then they won't perform their official duties."

"Well, what's the difference? Let them stop performing their governmental duties, and they'll be more free to work. Let them haul away the manure—they've piled up enough of it."

People came to Ivan to try lawsuits. One of them said: "That man stole my money."

And Ivan said, "Well, why not? That shows he needed it."

Everybody realized that he was a fool. Even his wife told him: "They say you're a fool."

"Well, why not?" he said.

His wife pondered and pondered, but she was a fool, too. "Why should I go against my husband?" she said. "Where the needle goes, the thread must follow."

So she took off her royal robes, put them away in a trunk, and went to the mute girl to learn how to work. She learned, and began helping her husband.

And all the clever people left Ivan's realm. Only the fools remained. Nobody had any money. They lived, worked, fed themselves, and fed all the good people.

X

Now the Old Devil waited and waited to hear from the imps how they had undone the three brothers, but there was no news. So he went to find out for himself. He looked and looked, but didn't find anything anywhere except three holes. Well, he thought, it is plain to see that they did not succeed.

He started investigating, but the three brothers were

no longer in their old places. He located them in their various kingdoms, all living and reigning. The Old Devil was highly incensed. Very well, then, he thought, I'll take care of this matter myself!

First he went to see Tsar Semyon. But the Old Devil did not keep his own form: he changed himself into an army commander first.

"I've heard, Tsar Semyon," he said, "that you are a great soldier. I myself am well skilled in such matters, and would like to serve you."

Tsar Semyon began to question him, and saw that he was a clever man; so he took him into his service.

The new commander began to teach Semyon how to build up a strong army. "In the first place," he said, "you'll have to draft more soldiers—otherwise you'll have a lot of no-good idlers in your realm. You must draft all of the young men without exception. Then you'll have an army five times bigger than it is now. In the second place, you must get new small arms and artillery. I will provide you with small arms that will fire a hundred bullets at once, so that they scatter like peas. And I will provide you with artillery pieces whose fire will simply incinerate things. Men, horses, walls, or whatever—all will go up in flames."

Tsar Semyon paid heed to his new army commander. He gave orders that all young men without exception should be drafted into the army; and he had new munitions plants built. He had new firearms and cannons manufactured, and immediately went to war with the king of a neighboring country. As soon as the other troops came forth to meet his, Tsar Semyon commanded his soldiers to fire their bullets and unleash their artillery on them. In an instant, half of the troops were crippled or incinerated. The neighboring king took fright, surrendered, and handed over his realm. Tsar Semyon was delighted.

"Now," said he, "I will conquer the king of India."

But the king of India had heard about Tsar Semyon and adopted all his new ideas, adding a few of his own. In addition to the young men, he drafted unmarried women besides, and his army grew even larger than Tsar Semyon's. In addition to copying all of Tsar Semyon's small arms and artillery, he had thought up the idea of flying through the air and hurling bombs from above.

Tsar Semyon set out to wage war on the king of India, thinking he would do battle in the same way as before. But what works once doesn't always work twice. The king of India, even before Semyon's troops could come within firing range, sent his women soldiers through the air to hurl down bombs from above. The women sprayed bombs on Semyon's army like borax on cockroaches. The whole army took flight, and Semyon was left alone. The king of India took over Semyon's empire, and Semyon the Soldier escaped as best he could.

Having finished off this particular brother, the Old Devil went on to Tsar Taras. He turned himself into a merchant, and settled in Taras's realm. There he set up a business, and began spending money freely, paying the highest prices for everything. Everybody in the country rushed to get some of his money. They got so much money that they settled their debts and even began paying their taxes on time.

Tsar Taras was delighted. Thanks to this merchant, he told himself, I'll have even more money than before, and my life will be better than ever.

And Tsar Taras began to dream up new schemes. He decided to build himself a new palace. He notified the people that they should bring him lumber and stone and come to work on the project; and he offered high prices

for everything, thinking they would come in flocks to work for his money, as before. But what do you think? They all took their lumber and stone to the merchant, and the workmen all flocked to him. Tsar Taras offered higher rates, but the merchant went still higher. Tsar Taras had a lot of money, but the merchant had even more; and he outbid the royal offer. The Tsar's palace was started, but never completed.

Tsar Taras had planned a park for himself. When autumn came, he sent for people to come and plant the trees and shrubs. But nobody came: everybody was busy digging a pond for the merchant.

Winter came. Tsar Taras decided to buy some sables for a new fur coat. He sent a man to buy them; but the man came back and said, "There aren't any sables. The merchant has all the furs. He paid a higher price, and he's made rugs out of the sables."

Tsar Taras needed to buy some stallions. He sent some men out to buy them; but they came back and said the merchant now had all the good stallions: he was using them to carry water for his pond.

So all of the Tsar's enterprises came to a standstill. All of the people were working for the merchant, not the Tsar. Their only dealings with him was when they paid him their taxes—in money they had got from the merchant.

Tsar Taras had amassed so much money he didn't know where to put it, yet life was becoming miserable for him. He had long ago stopped dreaming up schemes and just wanted to survive somehow; but he couldn't manage even that. There was a shortage of everything. His cooks and coachmen and other servants all left him and went to the merchant's. He even began to run out of food. When he sent to the market for something or other, there never was any: the merchant had bought up everything. Only one thing kept coming the Tsar's way: money from taxes.

Tsar Taras waxed furious: he banished the merchant from his realm. But the merchant settled directly across the border. Just as before, the merchant's money attracted everything to him and away from the Tsar.

The Tsar was in a really bad way. He hadn't eaten for days; and rumor had it that the merchant was boasting he was going to buy the Tsar's wife. Tsar Taras got panicky and didn't know which way to turn.

Semyon the Soldier came to him and said, "I need your help. The king of India defeated me."

But Tsar Taras, too, was at the end of his rope. "I haven't eaten for two days myself," he said.

XI

Having polished off both brothers, the Old Devil turned to Ivan. He changed himself into an army commander, went to see Ivan, and began trying to persuade him to raise an army. "It is not fitting," said he, "that a tsar should have no army. You have only to order me, and I will gather soldiers from among your people and form an army."

Ivan heard him out. "Well, why not?" he said. "Go ahead. But teach them to play their tunes a little better. That's what I like."

The Old Devil went through Ivan's realm trying to recruit volunteers. He announced that all who came to get their heads shaved and join the army would be given a bottle of vodka and a red cap.

Ivan's fools just laughed. "We have all the liquor we want," they said. "We make it ourselves. And our women make us all the different kinds of caps we want. They even make caps of many colors, with tassels to boot."

So nobody would enlist. The Old Devil came to Ivan and said: "Your fools won't volunteer. We'll have to bring them in by force."

"Well, why not?" Ivan said. "Go ahead and use force."

So the Old Devil announced that all of the fools had to come and enlist as soldiers, and that whoever did not would be put to death by Ivan.

The fools came to the commander and said: "You tell us that if we don't enlist as soldiers our tsar will put us to death. But you don't tell us what will happen to us in the army. They say soldiers get killed to death."

"Yes, that does happen."

When the fools heard this, they grew stubborn. "We won't enlist," they said. "It's better to be killed at home if it's going to happen one way or the other."

"You're fools!" said the Old Devil. "Such fools! A soldier may or may not get killed. But if you don't enlist, Tsar Ivan will be sure to have you killed."

The fools thought it over and went to see Tsar Ivan the Fool and ask him about it. "An army commander came," they said, "and ordered all of us to join the army. 'If you go into the army,' he told us, 'you may not get killed. But if you don't join, Tsar Ivan will be sure to have you killed.' Is that true?"

Ivan laughed. "How could I, all by myself, put all of you to death? If I weren't a Fool, I could explain it to you. But I don't understand it myself."

"All right, then," they said. "We won't go."

"Well," said Ivan, "what's the difference? Don't go."

So the fools went to the army commander and said they wouldn't enlist.

The Old Devil saw that his plan wasn't working. He went to the king of Cockroachia and talked himself into his favor. "Let's go to war," he said, "and conquer Tsar Ivan. He doesn't have any money; but he has lots of grain and livestock and other things."

The king of Cockroachia went to war. He raised a big army, put the rifles and cannon into good working order, and marched to the border of Ivan's country.

People came to Ivan and said, "The king of Cockroachia is coming to make war on us."

"Well," said Ivan, "what's the difference? Let him come."

The Cockroachian king crossed the border with his army and sent scouts ahead to reconnoiter.

They looked and looked, but they couldn't find any army. They waited and waited, thinking surely it would show up somewhere. But there wasn't a sign of an army —there was nobody they could fight.

The king of Cockroachia sent troops to capture the villages. They entered one village, and out ran the fools, men and women alike, gaping at the soldiers in astonishment. The soldiers began taking away the fools' grain and cattle. The fools just handed everything over, and not a one of them put up a fight.

The troops went into the next village, and the same thing happened. They marched on for another day, and another, and everywhere the same thing happened: they handed over everything; not a single one put up a fight; and they even invited the soldiers to stay. "Dear friends," they said, "if life is not good in your country, come and live here with us."

The soldiers marched on and on, but they never met up with an army: just people living and feeding themselves and others, never resisting—just inviting them to stay.

The soldiers became bored. They went to their Cockroachian king and said, "We can't fight here. Take us somewhere else. A war would be fine, but this is like slicing jelly. We can't go on with this campaign."

The king of Cockroachia flew into a rage. He commanded his soldiers to overrun the country, lay waste

the villages and houses, burn the grain, and slaughter
the livestock. "If you disobey my orders," he said, "all
of you will be put to death."

The soldiers were frightened and began to carry out
the king's orders. They burned houses and grain, and
slaughtered the livestock. But still the fools did not de-
fend themselves: all they did was weep. The old men
wept, the old women wept, and the little children wept.
"Why do you want to hurt us?" they asked. "Why are
you foolishly destroying good things? If you need them,
why don't you just take them?"

The soldiers couldn't bear it any longer. They refused to go on, and the army fell apart.

XII

The Old Devil also went away, having failed to undo
Ivan with the soldiers.

He turned himself into a fine gentleman and came
back to settle in Ivan's country. His plan now was to
undo Ivan the same way he had undone Taras the Big-
Belly: with money.

"I want to do you a favor;" he told Ivan, "to teach
you some common sense. I'll build a house here, and
set up a business."

"Well, why not?" said Ivan. "Go ahead."

The fine gentleman spent the night there; and the
next morning he appeared in the public square. He produced a big bag of gold and a sheet of paper. "All you
people," he said, "live like pigs. I want to show you

how to live properly. You build me a house according to this plan, and I'll supervise your work and pay you in gold coin."

He showed them the gold. The fools were amazed. They had never used money; instead, they bartered or paid one another by working. They marveled at the gold. "Those are pretty little things," they said.

And they began to exchange their labor and other things for the gentleman's gold pieces. The Old Devil started spending his gold freely, as he had done in Taras' kingdom; and the people began trading all kinds of things, and doing all kinds of work, for his gold.

The Old Devil was elated. Things are coming along fine, he thought. Now I'll fix the Fool the way I did Taras. I'll buy him out of the running—innards and all!

But no sooner had the fools garnered their gold pieces, than they gave them away to the women for necklaces. The girls plaited them into their braids, and the children played with them in the streets. They all had plenty of them, and they wouldn't take any more. Meantime, the fine gentleman's mansion was not yet half built, and his livestock and grain provisions for the coming year had not yet been taken care of. So he sent word that he wanted people to come and work for him, to haul in grain, and bring in livestock; and that for every product or every job done, he would pay lots of gold.

But nobody came to work for him, and nobody brought anything to him. A little boy or girl might occasionally stop by with an egg to trade in for gold; but otherwise nobody came, and he began to run out of food. The fine gentleman got very hungry and went through the village trying to buy something for his supper. He went to a peasant's house and offered gold for a hen, but the housewife wouldn't take it. "I have plenty of it already," she said.

He went to a poor old woman's and offered gold coins for a herring. "I don't need any of them, kind sir," said she. "I have no children I could give them to as toys, and besides I already have three coins I picked up as curiosities."

He went to an old peasant for bread. But the old peasant wouldn't take any money either.

"I don't need it," he said. "But if you're asking in the name of Christ, just wait a minute and I'll tell my old woman to cut you a slice."

The Old Devil spat and fled from the peasant. Let alone actually begging *in the name of Christ,* just hearing the words hurt him worse than a knife-stab.

And so he got no bread, either. All the people had all the money they needed. Wherever the Old Devil went, nobody would give anything for money. They all said, "Bring something else to trade, or come and do some work, or else take some food in the name of Christ." But the Old Devil had nothing but money, and he didn't want to work, and he couldn't possibly accept charity in the name of Christ.

He became furious. "I will give you money," he told the fools. "What more do you want? With money you can buy anything and hire any workman."

But they wouldn't listen. "No," they said, "we don't need it. We don't have any bills or taxes to pay, so what do we need money for?"

So the Old Devil went to bed without his supper.

Ivan the Fool heard about all this business. Some people came to him and asked: "What shall we do? There's this fine gentleman who appeared among us: he likes good things to eat and drink; he likes to wear fine clothes; but he doesn't like to work, and he won't beg in the name of Christ. All he does is offer gold pieces to everybody. People used to give him everything he needed; but now they have enough gold pieces and won't give him anything more. What should we do with him? He might starve to death."

Ivan listened to their story, and then said: "Well, after all," he said, "he has to be fed. Let him go from farm to farm, like a shepherd."

There was no other choice for him: the Old Devil had to start making the rounds of the farms.

Eventually he came to Ivan's house. He arrived at supper-time, and Malanya the Mute was preparing supper. Often before, she had been tricked by lazy people. Since they hadn't been working, they could get there for supper before the others; and then they'd eat up all the porridge. So she had learned to recognize loafers by the palms of their hands. If a man had calluses on his hands, she would seat him at the table; if not, he'd have to wait for the scraps.

The Old Devil sidled up to the table; but the mute girl seized him by the hands and took a look. There were no calluses: his hands were clean and smooth, with long fingernails. She grunted and dragged him away from the table.

But Ivan's wife said to him, "You must excuse us, fine sir. My sister-in-law doesn't let people sit at the table unless they have callused hands. Just wait a little, and when the others have eaten you can have what's left."

The Old Devil was insulted that at the Tsar's house they were making him eat along with the pigs. He said to Ivan, "That's a stupid law you have in your realm— that everybody has to work with his hands. Do you think it's only with their hands that people work? What do you suppose clever people work with?"

"How should we fools know?" Ivan answered. "We're all used to working mostly with our hands and our backs."

"That's because you're fools. But I'll teach you how to work with your heads. Then you'll realize it's more profitable to work with your head than your hands."

Ivan was astonished. "Well," said he, "it's no wonder we're called fools!"

"However," the Old Devil went on, "it's not so easy —working with your head. You refused to let me eat just now, because I didn't have calluses on my hands. But what you don't realize is that it's a hundred times harder to work with your head. Sometimes your head even splits."

Ivan thought about it a minute, "But then why, my dear friend," said he, "do you make it so hard on yourself? There's nothing easy about getting your head split, that's for sure. You'd be better off doing easy work —with your hands and your back."

Said the Old Devil, "Why do I make it hard on myself? Because I feel sorry for your fools. If I didn't make it hard on myself, you'd remain fools all your lives. But now that I've worked with my head, I can teach you how."

Ivan was very impressed. "You teach us," he said. "And then whenever our hands wear out, we can switch to our heads."

So the Old Devil promised to teach them.

Ivan announced throughout his realm that a fine gentleman had arrived who would teach them all how to work with their heads; and that a man could work more profitably with his head than with his hands, so everybody should come and learn how.

Now a high tower had been built in Ivan's realm, with a straight stairway on the outside, leading up to a lookout platform on the top. Ivan took the gentleman up there so that he would be in full view.

The gentleman stood atop the tower and began to

speak. The fools gathered around and gaped. They thought the gentleman would actually demonstrate how to work with your head without using your hands. But all the Old Devil did was talk—explaining how to live without doing any work.

The fools didn't understand a word of it. They watched a bit longer, and then went off to attend to their own business.

The Old Devil stood on top of the tower for one whole day, and then another—talking constantly. He got hungry. But it never occurred to the fools to bring some bread to the tower for him. They figured that if he could work better with his head than with his hands, it would be no trick at all for his head to provide him with bread.

The Old Devil stood up there on the tower for another whole day, still talking. People would come and take a look, then go away. Ivan asked, "Well, how is the gentleman doing? Has he started working with his head yet?"

"Not yet," they told him. "He's still jabbering."

The Old Devil stood on top of the tower for one more day, and began to grow weak. He staggered, and struck his head on a pillar. One of the people saw him topple, and told Ivan's wife. She ran out to the field where her husband was plowing. "Come and look!" she told him. "They say the gentleman has begun to work with his head."

Ivan marveled. "Oh?" said he.

He turned his horse around and went to the tower. By the time he got there the Old Devil was already very weak from hunger and was staggering around, knocking his head against the pillars. Just as Ivan got there he stumbled and fell, crashing down the stairway head over heels, counting each step with his head.

"Well," said Ivan, "the fine gentleman was telling the truth when he said that sometimes his head splits. In his kind of work it isn't calluses you get—it's lumps on the head."

The Old Devil came tumbling down the stairway and rammed his head into the ground at the bottom. Ivan had started toward him to see how much work he had done, when suddenly the earth opened up and the Old Devil fell into it. Only a hole remained.

Ivan scratched himself. "Just look at that! How disgusting! Him again! But he must be the father of all the others—he's a big one"

Ivan still lives to this day, and everybody flocks to his realm to live. His brothers have come there, too, and he feeds them.

Whenever anybody comes and says, "Feed us," he says, "Well, why not? Make yourself at home—we have plenty of everything."

But there is this one custom in his realm: if you have calluses on your hands, you're welcome at the table; if you don't, you eat the scraps.

The Bear Hunt

*W*e were out bear hunting. The friend who was with me got a shot at a bear and wounded him, but in a fleshy part. There was a little blood left on the snow, but the bear had gone off.

Our hunting party gathered together there in the forest and began trying to figure out what we should do—whether we should go after the bear right away, or wait two or three days until the animal holed up somewhere.

We asked the two peasants who were acting as our guides if it would be possible to overtake the bear right then. One of them, an old man, said, "You can't do it. You'll have to wait until the bear has settled down. In about five days you'll be able to catch up with him. But if you go after him now you'll just scare him, and he won't hole up at all."

But the young guide disagreed with the old man, and said it was possible to overtake the bear right then and there. "In this snow," he said, "that bear won't get very far. He's a fat one, and he's probably lying down somewhere already. And if he isn't, I'll catch up with him on my skis."

My friend, though, was against going after the bear now. It was his opinion that we should wait.

So I said, "Let's not argue. You do what you want to, and I'll go along with Demyan here, and track him. If we catch up with him, fine. If we don't, it doesn't matter. There's nothing else to do today, and it's still early."

So that's what we did.

The rest of the party got into the sleigh and went back to the village. Demyan and I, having provided ourselves with some bread, remained in the forest.

When the others had gone, the two of us checked the condition of our rifles, tightened the belts of our fur coats, and started off, tracking the bear.

The weather was fine—cold and windless—but it was hard going on skis. The snow was deep and powdery, and in the forest it hadn't settled yet. Besides, there had been a light snowfall the night before. Our skis sank down a good six inches in it, and sometimes more.

The bear's tracks were plainly visible far up ahead. We could see how he had moved along, and places where he had sunk in up to his belly and threshed about in the snow. At first, going through the tall forest, we stayed close on the tracks. But when they led into a small grove of fir trees, Demyan stopped. "Have to cut away from the tracks," he said. "He's probably going to lie down in there. He's already been sitting—you can see by the snow. Let's leave the tracks and circle around him. Only we have to be quieter about it. Mustn't cough or shout, or we'll scare him."

We headed off to the left from the bear's tracks. When we had gone about five hundred paces, there they were up ahead of us again. We got back on them, and they led us out onto a road. We stopped at the road and tried to discover which side of it the bear had gone along. Here and there you could see where the bear had left the imprint of his whole paw and all his toes; in other places you could see the footprints left by a peasant wearing shoes made of rope fiber. We could see that the bear was going in the direction of the village.

We walked along the road. Demyan said, "It's no use keeping an eye on the road. We can tell from the snow along the sides whether he went off to the right or the left. He won't go into the village."

We went on down the road like that for about two thirds of a mile, and then up ahead of us we saw tracks going off to one side. When we took a close look at them, we saw something amazing. Instead of going from the road toward the forest, these tracks went from the forest toward the road! "That's another bear," I said. Demyan studied the tracks, and pondered for a moment. "No," he said, "it's the same one. But he's started to get tricky with us. He backed off the road." We followed the tracks for a little way, and it turned out that Demyan was right. The bear had backed away from the road for about ten paces, and gone behind a pine tree. There he had turned around and gone on straight ahead. Demyan stopped, and said, "Now we'll catch up with him for sure. This swamp is the only place left for him to lie down in. Let's go around it to the other side."

We started off on our detour, moving through a thick growth of spruce. I was already dead tired, and the going was getting harder. Every now and then I'd ski into a juniper bush and get tangled up. Or a little seedling spruce would catch me between the legs. Or maybe one of my skis would get twisted in an unusual way. Or else I'd hit a stump or a log under the snow. I took off my fur coat—the sweat was pouring off me. But Demyan was gliding along like a boat through the water. His skis seemed to go of their own accord. He never got entangled, and his skis never got twisted. He had even draped my fur coat over his shoulder, and all the time he was urging me on.

We made a detour of about two miles, which took us around the swamp. I was beginning to lag behind; my skis kept crossing, and my feet kept getting in the way. Suddenly, up ahead of me, Demyan stopped and waved one hand. I came up to him. He crouched down, pointed, and whispered to me, "See, that magpie over there on that pile of deadwood is chattering. The bird can sense him from a long way off. It's our bear."

We set off in a hurry, went for about another half mile or more, and came upon the old tracks. So we had made a circle around the bear, and he had remained in the middle of our encirclement.

We stopped, and I took off my cap and unbuttoned all my clothes. I was so hot I might have been in a steam bath; I was wet all over. Even Demyan had grown red, and was wiping his face with his sleeve. "Well, sir," he said, "we did it. Now it's time to take a little rest."

Sunset was in fact already upon us, its reddening glow visible through the trees. We sat down on our skis to rest, and got some bread and salt from the bag. I ate some snow first, and then the bread. It seemed to taste better than any bread I had ever eaten in all my life. We sat there for a while, and it started to grow dark. I asked Demyan if it were far to the village. "About eight miles," was the answer. "We'll make it there tonight, but now we have to rest a bit. Better put on your coat, sir, or you'll get cold."

Demyan broke off some spruce boughs, beat down the snow, and made us a bed. We lay down side by side, with our hands under our heads. I don't really remember when or how I fell asleep. I woke up about two hours later. Something had made a crackling sound.

I had slept so soundly that I had even forgotten where I was. I looked around me—how wonderful! Where am I? A kind of white palace above me, and white pillars, and the whole thing aglitter. I looked straight up and saw intricate designs in white, and between them a kind of steel-blue dome or vault, and sparkling lights of different colors. Then I looked around again and remembered that we were in the forest, that these were trees with snow and frost on them, and that the lights were stars twinkling in the sky and glimpsed through the boughs.

There had been a frost that evening. And now there was frost on the boughs, and frost on my fur coat, and Demyan was all over frost; tiny flakes of it were still drifting down from above. I woke Demyan. We put on our skis and set off. In the forest, all was still. Except when a tree cracked from the frost, and the sharp snapping sound rang through the woods, the only noise was that made by our skis as we pushed through the soft snow. Once only did something alive make a sound very near us, and then run away. I thought it was the bear. But when we reached the place where the sound had come from, we saw hare tracks. And we saw some nibbled aspen. The hares had been feeding here.

We emerged onto the road, untied our skis, and walked. It was easy going. Dragged behind us, on the packed-down snow, the skis slid this way and that, clattering; the snow crunched under our boots; and the cold frost clung to our faces like fluff. The stars seemed to be rushing down the boughs to meet us, first brightening and then fading out, as though the whole sky were shaking.

My friend was sleeping. I woke him up, and we told how we had caught up with the bear and flanked him. We instructed our host to get together some beaters by morning; then we had supper and went to bed.

I was so exhausted that I could have slept until dinner time, but my friend got me up. I jumped out of bed and looked around; my friend was already dressed and fussing with his rifle.

"And where is Demyan?"

"He went back to the woods a long time ago. He has already checked the encirclement and come back here on the run. And now he's ordered the beaters to get started."

I washed, dressed, and loaded my rifle. Then we got into the sleigh and started off.

The freezing cold had not let up. It was a windless day, and sunless; the sky was overcast, and sleet was falling.

After covering about two miles on the road, we came to the forest. Then we noticed some blue smoke curling up from a little hollow, and some people standing around; peasants and their women, equipped with clubs.

We got out of the sleigh and went over to them. The men were sitting down, frying potatoes, and laughing and joking with the women.

Demyan was with them. They got up, and he showed them where to take up their positions along the circular path we had made the day before. The peasants and their women stretched out in a line (there were about thirty persons in all, visible only above the waist) and then started moving into the forest. My friend and I followed them.

Although the path was already made, the going was hard. On the other hand, you couldn't really fall down, because it was like a passageway between two walls.

When he had gone about a third of a mile we saw

Demyan rushing toward us on his skis from the other side, waving his hand for us to come.

We went up to him, and he showed us our places. I took my position and looked around me.

To my left was a stand of tall spruce trees. I could see clearly through this grove for a long distance; beyond the trees loomed the dark figure of a beater. Just across from me was a thick growth of young spruce about the height of a man. The boughs of the trees, laden with snow, drooped and stuck together. In the middle of this grove the path, which led directly toward me, had filled in with snow. To my right was another thick stand of spruce at the end of which was a little clearing. It was in this clearing, I noticed, that Demyan had stationed my friend.

I inspected my two rifles, and cocked them. Then I began considering where it would be best for me to stand. About three paces behind me was a big pine tree. "I think I'd better stand by that pine tree," I told myself, "and prop one of the rifles against it." I made my way toward the pine, sinking into snow that came up over my knees. Once there, I stamped down the snow over an area about a yard and a half square, and took up my post. I held one rifle in my hands, having propped the other, cocked, against the tree. I pulled out my knife and then put it back in its case—just to make sure that I could pull it out easily.

I had just got all set when I heard Demyan's voice ringing through the woods: "He's started moving! He's on the move—on the move!" Immediately, the peasants forming the circle began to shout, in different voices, "He's on the move!"

"Ooooh!" The men cried out. And the women, in their thin voices, yelled, "Aieee! Eeeekh!"

The bear was encircled, and Demyan was chasing him. All around, people were shouting. Only my friend and I were silent, immobile, waiting for the bear. I stood there, watching and listening, my heart thumping heavily. I held on to the rifle as tightly as I could, and I shivered. Any moment now, I thought, he'll jump out. I'll take aim and shoot, and he'll fall.

Suddenly, to my left, I heard something come crashing down in the snow. But it was far away. I stared hard at the grove of tall spruce trees. About fifty paces away, behind the trees, something big and black was standing erect. I took aim and waited. I was asking myself, "Won't he run this way?" But even as I watched, he twitched his ears and turned to go the other way. I had glimpsed the whole of him in profile. What a strapping beast! All excited, I took aim. *Bang!* I heard my bullet hit a tree. I peered through the smoke. The bear had rushed back into the ring and hidden himself in the forest. Well, I thought, I'm washed out. There's no more chance that he'll run in my direction. My friend may get a crack at him, or he may break out through the beaters, but he won't come my way.

I stood there, reloaded my rifle, and listened. The men were shouting all around. But to the right, not far from my friend, a woman was yelling unexpectedly: "There he is! There he is! There he is! He's coming this way! He's coming this way! Oi, Oi! Aieee, aieee, aieee!"

Unquestionably, he was in full sight. Not having any more expectation that he would come my way, I looked over to my friend, on the right. I saw Demyan coming down the path toward him, without skis and holding a stick in his hand. He squatted down beside him and pointed with his stick, as though aiming. Then I saw my friend raise his rifle and take aim in the direction Demyan had indicated. He fired. *Bang!* Well, thought I, he got him. But when I looked, I noticed that my friend didn't run after the bear. He must have missed, I said to myself, or else he hit where it doesn't count. So now the bear will go back the other way, and he'll never come toward me.

But what was this? Suddenly right up ahead of me I heard something rushing along like a whirlwind, scattering the snow close to me, and panting. I looked up, and the bear was coming headlong toward me down the path through the thick spruce—plainly out of his mind with fear. I could see all of him at about five paces —the black chest, and the huge head with the reddish spot. He was rushing right at me, making the snow fly on all sides. And I could see from his eyes that he didn't see me, that out of sheer fright he was going as fast as he could and anywhere he could. The only trouble was, he was headed straight for my pine tree and me. I raised my rifle and shot, but he came still closer. I could see that I'd missed. But he didn't hear anything; he kept coming right at me. I lowered my gun until it was almost against his head. *Bang!* I hit him this time, but I didn't kill him.

He raised his head a little, laying his ears back, bared his teeth, and came for me. I reached for the other rifle. But no sooner had I grabbed it than he was on top of me. He knocked me down in the snow, and jumped over me. Well, I thought, I'm lucky. He's let me go. I started to get up, but felt something weighing me down, pinning me. He hadn't been able to control himself in his flight. He had jumped over me, but then he had turned around, and his whole chest came crashing down on mine.

I felt something heavy lying on me, sensed something warm on my face, and was aware he was about to take my whole head into his mouth. My nose was already in

his mouth; its smell of heat and blood came to me. His paws on my shoulders held me down, and I couldn't move. All I could do was bend my head down from his mouth toward his chest and avert my nose and eyes. But my nose and eyes were just what he was after. I could feel the teeth of his upper jaw catching my forehead just at the hairline, the lower jaw catching my cheekbone under the eyes, the setting of his teeth, and the beginning of the squeeze. Those teeth cut into my head like knives. I struggled, and broke free; but he was back at me in no time, gnawing like a dog—chomping and chomping. I wrenched free again, but again he started in. This is the end, I thought. Then suddenly I felt things ease up. And when I looked, he was gone. He'd jumped off me and run away.

When my friend and Demyan had seen that the bear had knocked me down in the snow and was gnawing at me, they had rushed over. My friend had tried to hurry, but he'd made a mistake: instead of keeping to the packed-down path he had come straight for me, and had fallen. While he was struggling out of the snow, the bear continued to gnaw at me. But Demyan, though he had no gun, but only a switch, ran down the path shouting, "He's eating the gentleman! He's eating the gentleman!" He ran right at the bear and shouted: "You're a bad one! What are you doing? Stop it! Stop it!"

The bear obeyed. He let me go, and ran off. When I stood up, there was blood on the snow, as though a sheep's throat had just been cut; and above my eyes my flesh was hanging in scraps. But in all the excitement I felt no pain.

My friend ran up, and the peasants gathered round. They examined my wound, and put snow on it. But I had forgotten about the wound. "Where is the bear?"

I asked. "Where did he go?" Suddenly we heard somebody yell, "There he is! There he is!" We looked, and saw the bear running at us again. We reached for our rifles, but he had gone past us before anyone could take a shot. He was in a frenzy, and eager to do some more gnawing. But when he saw how many people there were, he got frightened. From looking at his tracks we could tell that he was bleeding. We wanted to go after him, but my head had started aching. So we went into town to see a doctor.

The doctor stitched up my wounds, and they began to heal.

A month later we went after that same bear. But we didn't manage to get him. He never came out of the encirclement, but just went round and round, bellowing in a terrible voice.

It was Demyan who got him finally. The bear's lower jaw had been smashed by my shot, and one tooth had been knocked out.

He was a very big bear, and had a beautiful black coat. I had him stuffed, and I keep him in my room.

The wounds on my forehead have healed, and you can hardly see where they were.

God Sees the Truth
but Is in No
Hurry to
Reveal
It

*I*n the town of Vladimir there lived a young merchant by the name of Aksenov. He had two shops and his own house.

Aksenov was a handsome fellow with curly fair hair, always the liveliest one at a party, and the first to strike up a song. In his youth he drank a lot; and when he was tipsy he would get into fights. But when he got married he pretty much quit drinking, so that didn't happen so often.

One day in the summer Aksenov was going to the fair at Nizhny. As he was bidding goodbye to his family, his wife said, "Ivan Dmitriyevich, I wish you wouldn't go today. I had a bad dream about you."

Aksenov chuckled and said, "Are you still afraid that I'll go on a binge at the fair?"

"No," his wife replied, "I don't know myself what it is I'm afraid of. But I had such a bad dream: I dreamed that when you came back from town and took off your cap I saw your hair had turned completely gray."

Aksenov laughed outright. "That's a good sign. You just wait: I'll do well in my trading and bring you back some expensive gifts."

Then he said goodbye and left.

When he had gone half his journey he met up with another merchant he knew, and they stopped for the night. They drank tea together, and then went to bed in adjoining rooms. Aksenov did not like to sleep long.

He awakened in the middle of the night and, since it was easier traveling when it was cool, he woke up his coachman and told him to harness the horses. Then he went out to the hut back of the inn, settled with the innkeeper, and left.

When he had gone about another twenty-six miles he stopped at another inn. He had the horses fed, and then rested for a while. At dinner time he went out on the porch and ordered a samovar to be brought to him, then picked up a guitar and began to play. Suddenly a troika with jingling bells drove up. An official accompanied by two soldiers got out. The official came up to Aksenov and asked, "Who are you? Where are you from?"

Aksenov answered his questions, giving all the facts, and then asked, "Wouldn't you like to have some tea with me?" But the official kept on questioning him, asking where he had spent the night: alone or with another merchant? Had he seen the merchant the next morning? And why did he leave the inn so early?

Aksenov couldn't understand why he was being questioned about all those things. He related everything, just as it had happened, and then he asked, "But why are you interrogating me like this? I'm not some kind of a thief or highwayman. I'm traveling on my own business, and there's no reason for you to interrogate me."

The official called the soldiers over. "I'm the district police inspector," he said, "and I'm questioning you because the merchant who stayed at the inn with you last night has been murdered—his throat was slit. Show me your things! And you two: search this man!"

They went into Aksenov's room, brought out his suitcase and bag, and began to search them. Suddenly the inspector pulled a knife out of the bag and shouted, "Whose knife is this?"

Aksenov looked, and saw that the inspector had taken a bloodstained knife from his bag. He was frightened.

"Why is there blood on this knife?"

Aksenov tried to answer, but couldn't get the words out. "I . . . I don't know . . . I . . . knife . . . not mine."

Then the inspector said, "In the morning, the merchant was found in his bed with his throat cut. You are the only one who could have done it. That suite of rooms was locked from the inside, and nobody else but you had been in there. Besides which you had a bloodstained knife in your bag, and guilt is written all over your face. So tell me: How did you do it and how much money did you get?"

Aksenov swore that he hadn't killed the merchant; that he had not seen him again after they had drunk tea together; that the only money he had on him was his own eight thousand rubles; and that the knife was not his. But he stammered, his face was pale, and he shook all over with fear as though he were guilty.

The inspector called a soldier and told him to bind Aksenov and put him in a *telega*—a kind of springless carriage. When they lifted him into the *telega*, with his feet bound, Aksenov crossed himself and began to weep.

They confiscated his money and other personal possessions, and sent him to jail in a nearby town. They had inquiries made in Vladimir to find out what sort of a man Aksenov was; and all the merchants and other people in Vladimir reported that in his youth Aksenov had been given to drinking and carousing, but that he was a good person. Then he was brought to trial. The charges were that he had killed a merchant from Ryazan and stolen twenty thousand rubles.

His wife was overcome with grief, and didn't know where to turn. All of her children were very young, and one was still at the breast. She took all of them and went to the town where her husband was being held in jail. At first they wouldn't let her in. But she pleaded with the authorities, and finally they took her to her husband. When she saw him there among criminals, shackled and wearing convict's garb, she fell to the ground in a faint and did not recover for a considerable time. When she did, she gathered her children around, sat down beside him, and began to tell about things at home and ask him about everything that had happened to him.

"And what now?" she asked.

"We'll have to appeal to the Tsar. They can't let an innocent man perish."

His wife said that she had already addressed a petition to the Tsar, but it had not been allowed to reach him. Aksenov made no reply; he just stared at the ground.

"Remember that dream I had—when I dreamed your

hair turned gray? Well, there was something to it, because now your hair really has begun to turn gray. You
shouldn't have gone on that trip."

She began to run her fingers through his hair, saying,
"Vanya, my dearest, tell your wife the truth: did you
do it?"

"Then even you suspect me?" He covered his face
with his hands and began to weep.

A guard came in and said that his wife and children had to leave. And Aksenov bade goodbye to his family for the last time.

When his wife had left, he began thinking over what they had told each other. And when he thought again of how she, too, had suspected him and asked him whether he killed the merchant, he said to himself, "I see now that only God can know the truth. It is to Him alone that I must appeal, and from Him alone that I may hope for mercy." And from that time on he ceased to submit any petitions, and he ceased to hope, but only prayed to God.

Aksenov was sentenced to a flogging and banishment to a prison camp.

The sentence was duly carried out. He was given a flogging with a knout; then, when the wounds had healed over, he was sent along with other convicts to Siberia.

Aksenov lived for twenty-six years in the Siberian prison camp. The hair on his head turned white as snow; his beard grew long, thin, and gray. There was nothing left of his former gay spirits. He became hunched, walked slowly, said very little, and never laughed. He prayed often.

In prison he learned how to make boots, and with the money earned in this way he bought *Lives of the Saints* and read it when there was light enough in his cell. On holy days he went to the prison chapel where he read the Acts of the Apostles and sang in the choir, since his voice was still good. The prison authorities liked Aksenov for his humility, and his fellow convicts respected him and called him "Grandpa" or "God's Fool." When the prisoners had a petition to submit to the officials, they always sent Aksenov to see them. And when a quarrel arose among any of the convicts, they always asked him to act as judge.

None of Aksenov's family ever wrote to him, and he didn't even know whether his wife and children were alive.

One day some new convicts were brought to the prison camp. In the evening, all the old inmates gathered around the new ones and started asking them what town or village they were from and what they had been sent to prison for. Aksenov, too, sat down on a bunk near the new arrivals and listened to their stories, his eyes on the floor.

One of the new convicts was a tall, sturdy old man of about sixty with a short gray beard. He was telling why he had been arrested. "The way it was, fellows—I was sent here for no reason at all," he said. "I'd unhitched a horse from a coachman's sleigh. They grabbed me and said I'd stolen it. 'No,' I told them, 'I just wanted to get to where I was going faster. Anyway, I'd let the horse go. And besides, the coachman was a friend of mine. Everything's above board,' I said. 'No,' they said. 'You're a thief.' Well, I am; but they didn't know what I really stole, or where. I've pulled off jobs that should have landed me here a long time ago, but they never could catch me. And now they send me here illegally! But then I'm lying: I've been in Siberia before. Not for long, though."

"Where are you from?" asked one of the convicts.

"From Vladimir—my family are townspeople there. Semyonovich is the name—Makar Semyonov."

Aksenov raised his head and asked: "Tell me, Semyonov, did you ever hear anything in Vladimir about a merchant family called Aksenov? Are they alive?"

"Who hasn't heard of them? They're rich merchants, even though the father's in Siberia. He's the same kind as the rest of us here, it looks like. But what about you, Grandpa? What are you in for?"

Aksenov didn't like to talk about his own misfortune. He sighed and said, "For my sins I have spent twenty-six years at hard labor."

"What kind of sins?" asked Semyonov.

"The kind that brought me this punishment," Aksenov said, and didn't want to tell any more. But the other convicts told the new arrival why Aksenov had been sent to Siberia. They told him of how someone had murdered a merchant at an inn and then planted the knife on Aksenov; and how the latter had been falsely convicted.

When Semyonov heard this he looked at Aksenov, slapped his hands on his knees, and said, "I can't believe it! I just can't believe my eyes! Grandpa, you've grown a lot older!"

They started asking him why he was so surprised and where he had seen Aksenov before, but Semyonov didn't answer their questions. All he said was, "It's a miracle the way you run across people!"

When he heard those words, it occurred to Aksenov that perhaps this man knew something about who had murdered the merchant. "Semyonov," he asked, "did you hear something about the case? Or have you seen me before?"

"Naturally I heard about the case. News travels fast. But it happened a long time ago, and what I heard about it I've forgotten."

"Did you perhaps hear who it was that murdered the merchant?" Aksenov asked.

Semyonov laughed and said, "That's clear enough: the man who killed him was the owner of the bag where they found the knife. Or else, if somebody *did* plant a knife on you—well, a thief's not a thief until he's caught. But for that matter, how could anybody slip a knife into your bag? It was right next to your head. You would have heard him."

As soon as Aksenov heard these words he realized that it was this man who had murdered the merchant. He got to his feet and went away.

All that night he was unable to sleep. He became very depressed, and began to summon up images. He saw his wife as she had been that day when she bid him goodbye as he left for the fair. He saw her as clearly as though she were standing there before him: saw her face and her eyes, and heard her voice as she talked to him and laughed. He saw his children as they were then— still small, one in a little coat, the other at the breast. And he remembered himself as he was then—young and fun-loving. He remembered how he had sat on the porch at the inn where they had arrested him, playing the guitar, and how happy he had been then. He remembered, too, the execution dock where they had flogged him, the hangman, the twenty-six long years of prison life. And he remembered that now he was very old. He was so heartsick that he was ready to kill himself.

And all because of that evil man, he thought.

Aksenov conceived such a hatred for Semyonov that he wanted to avenge himself even at the cost of his own life. All night long he recited prayers, but he couldn't calm his feelings. The next day he refused to come near Semyonov and wouldn't even look at him.

Two weeks passed in this way. Aksenov couldn't sleep at night; he was so despondent he didn't know which way to turn.

One night he was wandering through the prison barracks when he noticed that dirt was being tossed up from under one of the bunks, making a little pile. He stopped and looked. Suddenly Semyonov came out from under the bunk and threw a frightened glance at Aksenov. The latter tried to go on past and avoid him. But Semyonov grabbed him by the arm and told him he was digging a tunnel under the wall; and that every day, when the convicts were taken out to work, he carried out the dirt in his boot-tops and scattered it in the street. He added, "Just keep mum about this, Grandpa, and I'll take you along. But if you tell on me, I'll get flogged. As for you—I won't let you get away: I'll kill you."

When he looked at this evil man who had wronged him, Aksenov trembled all over with rage. Jerking his arm away, he said, "There's no reason why I should leave here, and no reason why you should kill me: you did that long ago. As for whether I'll report you—that will happen as it may."

The next day, when the convicts were being taken out to work, the guards noticed Semyonov scattering dirt. They searched the barracks, and found the hole he had dug. The warden came in and started asking everybody who had dug the hole. They all denied doing it. Those who knew that Semyonov had done it didn't tell on him, because they knew he would be flogged almost to death.

Then the warden turned to Aksenov, knowing he was a just man, and asked, "Grandpa, you speak the truth. Tell me before God who did this?"

Semyonov stood there as though nothing had happened, watching the warden and never once glancing at Aksenov. Aksenov's hands and lips were trembling, and for a long time he couldn't get a word out. He was thinking: If I don't give him away . . . But why should I forgive him when he ruined my life? Let him pay for my sufferings. But if I tell on him, they'll flog him for sure. And what if I suspected him wrongly? Besides, would it make things any easier for me?

Once again the warden said, "Well, Grandpa, tell me the truth: who was digging?"

Aksenov glanced at Semyonov and said: "I can't tell you, Your Honor. God has not commanded me to, and I won't. You can do whatever you want with me."

No matter how hard the warden tried with him, Aksenov wouldn't say anything more. So they never found out who had dug the hole.

The next night, Aksenov was lying on his bunk and was almost asleep, when he heard someone come up and sit on the foot of the bunk. He peered through the darkness and recognized Semyonov. Aksenov said, "What more do you want of me? What are you doing here?"

Semyonov was silent. Aksenov raised himself up and said, "What do you want? Get away from here or I'll call a guard."

Semyonov leaned over close to Aksenov and whispered: "Forgive me, Ivan Dmitrich!"

"Forgive you for what?"

"I killed the merchant, and I planted the knife on you. I was going to kill you, too, but then I heard some noise outside. I slipped the knife into your bag and crawled out through the window."

Aksenov didn't answer—not knowing what to say. Semyonov slid off the bunk, bowed his head to the floor, and said, "Forgive me! I'll confess that I murdered the merchant, and they'll pardon you. Then you can go home."

Aksenov said, "It's easy for you to talk, but how I have suffered! Where could I go now? My wife is dead, and my children have forgotten me. There's no place for me to go."

Semyonov did not get up. He beat his head on the floor, and said, "Ivan Dmitrich, forgive me! When they flogged me with a knout, it was easier for me than it is now—just looking at you . . . And on top of everything, you took pity on me and didn't turn me in. Forgive me, for the love of Christ! Forgive an evildoer who is damned!" And he started to sob.

When Aksenov heard Semyonov weeping, he himself began to weep, and he said, "God will forgive you. Perhaps I am a hundred times worse than you!"

Suddenly, a weight seemed to have been lifted from his soul. He ceased to yearn for his home, and he lost all desire to get out of prison: all he thought of was his final hour.

Semyonov disregarded Aksenov's advice and confessed to the murder. But by the time the order for Aksenov's release arrived, he was already dead.

β